NIGHT FIGHTERS IN FRANCE

Other Titles In The SAS Operation Series

Behind Iraqi Lines
Mission to Argentina
Sniper Fire in Belfast
Desert Raiders
Samarkand Hijack
Embassy Siege
Guerrillas in the Jungle
Secret War in Arabia
Colombian Cocaine War
Invisible Enemy in Kazakhstan
Heroes of the South Atlantic
Counter-insurgency in Aden
Gambian Bluff
Bosnian Inferno
Death on Gibraltar
Into Vietnam
For King and Country
Kashmir Rescue
Guatemala – Journey into Evil
Headhunters of Borneo
Kidnap the Emperor!
War on the Streets
Bandit Country
Days of the Dead

Night Fighters in France

SHAUN CLARKE

HARPER

This novel is entirely a work of fiction.
The names, characters and incidents portrayed in it are the work of the author's imagination. Any resemblance to actual persons, living or dead, events or localities is entirely coincidental.

Harper
An imprint of HarperCollins*Publishers*
1 London Bridge Street,
London SE1 9GF
www.harpercollins.co.uk

This paperback edition 2016
1

First published by 22 Books/Bloomsbury Publishing plc 1994

A catalogue record for this book is available from the British Library

ISBN: 978 0 00 815524 7

Set in Sabon by Born Group using Atomik ePublisher from Easypress

Printed and bound in Great Britain

Prelude

Operation Overlord, the Allied invasion of Europe, commenced on the night of 5 June 1944 with the concentrated bombing of German positions on the north coast of France by 750 heavy bombers, an onslaught against the Normandy defence batteries by hundreds of medium bombers, the clearing of broad sea highways thirty miles long by 309 British, 22 American and 16 Canadian minesweepers, and landings by parachute and glider in the vicinity of the east bank of the Caen canal and astride the Cherbourg peninsula. Fires were already burning all along the coast of Normandy, acting as beacons to the invasion fleet, when, just as dawn broke on D-Day, 6 June, Fortresses and Liberators of the US 8th and 9th Air Forces, covered by an umbrella of fighters, dropped 2400 tons of bombs on the British beaches and nearly 2000 tons on the American beaches.

Shortly after dawn, the warships heading for Normandy opened fire with their big guns, covering the coastline with spectacular flashes and clouds of brownish cordite while the British 'Hunt'-class destroyers raced in to engage the enemy's shore batteries. To the west, American destroyers were doing the same, with the heavier guns of their battleships hurling fourteen, fifteen and sixteen-inch shells on to the beaches and the German fortifications beyond them. The final 'softening up' was achieved by rocket-firing boats which disappeared momentarily behind sheets of flame as their deadly payload rained down on the beaches, adding to the general bedlam by causing more mighty explosions, which threw up mushrooms of flying soil and swirling smoke.

At 0630 hours American forces swarmed on to the western shores, where a broad bay sweeps round to Cherbourg. They were followed fifty minutes later by British and Canadian troops, put ashore by more than 5000 landing-craft and 'Rhino' ferries on the eastern beaches. Many of the assault craft were caught by sunken angle-irons and, with their bottoms ripped open, foundered before they made the shore; others were blown up by mines.

Nevertheless the men, each heavily burdened with steel helmet, pack and roll, two barracks bags, rations, two cans of water, gas mask, rifle and bayonet, bandoliers of ammunition, hand-grenades and, in many cases, parts of heavy weapons such as machine-guns and mortars – a total weight never less than 132lb – continued to pour ashore on both the eastern and western fronts, advancing into the murderous rifle and machine-gun fire of the Germans still holed up in their concrete bunkers overlooking the beaches. Likewise savaged by a hail of enemy gunfire were the Royal Engineers and American sappers, who continued bravely to explode buried German mines to create 'safe' paths for the advancing Allied troops.

Within minutes, the beaches, obscured in a pall of smoke, were littered with dead bodies and black shell holes. The sounds of machine-guns and mortars increased the already appalling din. Out at sea, the guns of Allied cruisers, battleships and destroyers continued a bombardment that would account for 56,769 shells of various calibres. Simultaneously, the Air Force continued to pound the enemy positions: more than 1300 Liberators and Fortresses, escorted by fighters, bombed the German positions for another two and a half hours.

By evening the Germans overlooking the beach had been pushed well back and Allied forces were as far as six to eight miles inland. While British Commandos and American Rangers were having spectacular successes on their separate fronts, a Royal Marine Commando, even after the loss of five of its fourteen landing-craft, fought through Les Roquettes and La Rosière, quelled several German machine-gun and mortar nests, and finally captured Port-en-Bessin. There, making contact with the Americans, it linked up the whole Allied front in Normandy and paved the way for the major push through France.

Strategically vital bridges, locks and canals soon fell to the Allies and in many small towns and villages French men and women emerged from rubble and clouds of dust to wave the tricolour and rapturously greet their liberators.

Even though German resistance was heavy, by the evening of the first day a bridgehead twenty-five miles wide had been established, forming a continuous front, with American forces in the Cotentin peninsula and just east of the River Vire, and Canadian and British troops on the left flank. To the east, British troops advanced to within three miles of Caen, while to the west US forces penetrated to a depth of five miles south of Colleville and crossed the River Aure to the east of Trévières. Two days later, Isigny, six miles from Carentan, was captured. Carentan itself fell to US troops on the 12th.

Violent fighting broke out around Caen, with both sides changing positions constantly, but the Americans entered

St-Sauveur-le-Vicomte on the 16th, reached the main defences of Cherbourg on the 21st and, after fierce fighting, but with the aid of an intensive aerial bombardment and artillery fire, captured the town on the 27th, taking 20,000 German prisoners of war.

By this time, British troops had cut the road and railway between Caen and Villers-Bocage to reach the River Odon at a point some two miles north of Evrecy. A strong bridgehead was established which resisted the counter-attacks of eight Panzer and SS Panzer divisions. When the Germans retreated, the bridgehead was secured and enlarged.

On 3 July, having cleared the north-west tip of the Cotentin peninsula, the US 1st Army advanced in a blinding rainstorm on a wide front south of St-Sauveur-le-Vicomte. By the following day they had captured the high ground to the north of La Haye-du-Puits and, after eight days of fierce fighting, finally captured the town. Simultaneously, other US troops were battling their way up the steep, wooded slopes of the Forêt de Mont Castre and advancing down the Carentan-Périers road to force a passage across the Vire in the direction of St-Jean-de-Daye, which fell on the 8th. By the 11th they were advancing through waterlogged country to take up positions within three miles of the vital German communications centre of St Lô.

British and Canadian forces, meanwhile, had attacked eastwards towards Caen, and early on the 8th, after a concentrated bombardment from heavy and medium bombers, launched an attack that carried them to the outskirts of the town. Supported by sustained fire from massed artillery and British ships, they took the northern part of the town by nightfall.

St Lô fell to the US 1st Army on 18 July after eight days of bloody fighting. Following the capture of the northern part of Caen, the British 2nd Army, under Montgomery, launched an attack southeast of the town. Over 2000 British and American heavy and medium bombers dropped nearly 8000 tons of bombs in an area of little more than seventy square miles, blasting a 7000-yard-wide passage that enabled armoured formations to cross the River Orne by specially constructed bridges and drive strong wedges in the direction of Cagny and Bourguébus.

While this armoured advance was temporarily halted by a combination of determined enemy resistance and violent rainstorms, Canadian troops were successfully clearing the southern suburbs of Caen and British infantry were thrusting out eastwards towards Troarn to clear several villages in the area. A further Canadian attack across the Orne, west of Caen, resulted in the capture of Fleury and the clearing of the east bank of the river for three miles due south of the latter town.

A week after the British 2nd Army's offensive began, the US 1st Army attacked west of St Lô, captured Marigny and St-Gilles, then fanned out in three columns, west, south and south-west, to capture Canisy, Lessay, Périers and Coutances, and join up with US forces advancing from the east. By nightfall of the 30th, American armour had swept through Bréhal and, the following day, captured Avranches and Graville. Further east, Bérigny was captured.

Aiding the American success were two attacks in the British sector: one by the Canadians down the Caen-Falaise road, the other in the area of Gaumont, where, after a heavy air bombardment, a British armoured and infantry force secured Cahagnes and Le Bény-Bocage. Five more villages, including the strategically important Evrecy and Esquay, southwest of Caen, were captured on 4 August and Villers-Bocage, which was by now in ruins, the next day.

American armoured columns reached Dinan that same week, turned south and, heading for Brest, liberated several Breton towns *en route*. Rennes, the capital of Brittany, was captured on the 4th and the River Vilaine was reached two days later, sealing off the Brittany peninsula. The fall of Vannes, Lorient, St-Malo, Nantes and Angers soon followed, and US patrols had crossed the Loire by 11 August.

With British and Canadians, plus the 1st Polish Armoured Division, advancing from the north, and the Americans, along with the French 2nd Armoured Division, closing in from the west and south, a large part of the German 7th Army was almost surrounded. Their only escape route – the narrow Falaise-Argentan Gap – was sealed by the Americans advancing from Le Mans, which they had liberated on 9 August.

By 19 August, the Falaise Gap was closed and, after a terrible slaughter of German troops, whose dead choked the village streets and surrounding fields, the sad remnants of von Kluge's 7th Army were taken prisoner.

Four days earlier, on 15 August, General Eisenhower had taken command of the Allied Expeditionary Force, leaving Montgomery at the head of the 21st Army Group, which consisted of General Dempsey's British 2nd Army and General Crerar's 1st Canadian Army. Lieutenant-General Omar Bradley was at the head of the 12th Army Group, comprising General Hodge's US 1st Army and General Patton's 3rd Army. The latter was driving towards Dijon as other Allied forces advanced from the south.

To aid the advance of Patton's 3rd Army, the Allies planned airborne landings in the Orléans Gap, and to soften the enemy before the landings, they decided to drop a squadron of men and jeeps by parachute in the area of Auxerre, central France. The squadron's task would be to engage in a series of daring hit-and-run night raids against German positions to distract the enemy from the landings taking place elsewhere.

While the Allied advance was under way, the French Forces of the Interior (FFI) were seizing high ground in advance of the American armour and engaging in guerrilla warfare, to harass the Germans and protect Allied lines of communication. In central France, the Maquis – Frenchmen who had fled from the Germans and were living in makeshift camps in the forest – were conducting sabotage missions behind enemy lines. Among their tasks were blowing up bridges, putting locomotives out of action, derailing trains, and cutting long-distance underground communications cables between Paris and Berlin. Montgomery, knowing of these activities, decided that the men chosen for the parachute drop should establish a base and make contact with the Maquis.

The men deemed most suitable for this mission, known as Operation Kipling, were those of C Squadron, 1 SAS, based in Fairford, Gloucestershire. Formed in North Africa in 1941, 1 SAS had already gained a reputation for uncommon daring. That reputation would be put to the test over the weeks to come.

1

The men crowding into the briefing room in their heavily guarded camp near Fairford, Gloucestershire on 10 August 1944 were not ordinary soldiers. They were men of uncommon ability, members of the Special Air Service (1 SAS), which had been formed in North Africa in 1941 as a self-contained group tasked with clandestine insertion, long-range reconnaissance patrols behind enemy lines, and sabotage and intelligence-gathering missions, often with the Long Range Desert Group (LRDG).

Originally, 1 SAS had been conceived and formed by Lieutenant David Stirling, a former Scots Guard who, having joined No. 8 Commando, was promptly dispatched to the Middle East on attachment to Colonel Robert Laycock's Layforce. After taking part in many relatively unsuccessful, large-scale raids against German positions along the North African coast, Stirling became convinced that raids with small, specially trained units would be more effective. In the spring of 1941, hospitalized in Alexandria after a parachute accident, he passed the time by formulating his plans for just such a unit, based on the belief that 200 men operating as five-man teams could achieve the surprise necessary to destroy several targets on the same night. Subsequently, with the support of Deputy Chief of Staff General Neil Ritchie, L Detachment, Special Air Service Brigade, was born.

The new SAS Brigade's first raids behind enemy lines in November 1941, which involved parachute drops, were a complete failure. However, later raids against Axis airfields at Sirte, Tamit, Mersa Brega and Agedabia, during which the men were driven to their targets and returned to base by the highly experienced LRDG, were remarkably successful, gaining L Detachment a legendary reputation. By October 1942, when L Detachment was given full regimental status as 1 SAS, it had grown to include the 390 troops of the existing 1 SAS, the French Squadron of 94 men, the Greek Sacred Squadron of 114 men, the Special Boat Section of 55 men and the Special Interrogation Group.

Lieutenant Stirling was captured in January 1943, incarcerated in Gavi, Italy, from where he escaped no less than four times, then transferred to the German high-security prison at Colditz. In April 1943, while Stirling was embarking on a series of daring escapes from Gavi, the French and Greek Squadrons were returned to their respective national armies, the Special Boat Section became a separate unit, the Special Boat Squadron (SBS), under the command of Major Jellicoe, and 1 SAS became the Special Raiding Squadron. In May 1943 2 SAS came into existence and, later that year, the Special Raiding Squadron reverted to the title of 1 SAS. Finally, in January 1944, the SAS Brigade was formed under the umbrella of 1st Airborne Corps. It consisted of 1 and 2 SAS, 3 SAS (3 French Parachute Battalion), 4 SAS (4 French Parachute Battalion), 5 SAS (Belgian Independent Parachute Company), HQ French Demi-Brigade, F Squadron, GHQ Liaison Regiment and 20 Liaison HQ, which was the SAS link with the Free French.

The men crowding into the briefing room at Fairford, however, were the British founder members of the SAS Brigade, having joined it in North Africa in 1941 and taken part in its first daring raids. The 'Head Shed' in charge of the briefing and now taking up his position in front of the covered blackboard on a raised platform was the squadron commander, Captain Patrick 'Paddy' Callaghan, No. 3 Commando, an accomplished boxer and Irish rugby international who had, at the time of the formation of L Detachment, been languishing in a military-police cell in Cairo, waiting to be court-martialled. Though normally an amiable, courteous man, Callaghan had a fiery temper and had often landed in trouble because of it. Nevertheless, he was one of the most able officers in the SAS, often mentioned in dispatches for his bravery in action. Thus, though he had not been promoted since 1941, his abilities had been officially recognized when his superiors put him in charge of C Squadron.

Standing beside the heavily built Captain Callaghan was his slim, handsome second in command, former Lieutenant, now Captain, Derek 'Dirk' Greaves. Like Stirling, Greaves had been a member of No. 9 Commando, posted to General Wavell's Middle Eastern Army on attachment to Layforce. With Layforce he had taken part in raids against the Axis forces in Rhodes, Crete, Syria, around Tobruk and all along the seaward side of Libya's Cyrenaica Desert, before being wounded, meeting Lieutenant Stirling in the Scottish Military Hospital in Alexandria and becoming his right-hand man in the formation of L Detachment. Single when with Layforce, he had since married his Scottish fiancée, Mary Radnor, and now missed her dreadfully, though he took comfort from the knowledge that she was living safely in the family home in Edinburgh, and now eight months pregnant with their first child.

'All right, men, quieten down!' Captain Greaves shouted. 'We haven't got all day!'

When the spirited babble continued even as Captain Callaghan was taking up his position in the middle of the dais, Sergeant Ralph Lorrimer bawled: 'Shut your mouths and let the boss speak! Are you men deaf, or what?'

Formerly of the Dorset Regiment, then with the LRDG, an expert in desert tracking and warfare, but also unbeatable with the Browning 12-gauge autoloader, Lorrimer had been approached by Stirling and Greaves to join L Detachment when he was spending his leave in Tiger Lil's brothel in Cairo's notorious Sharia el Berka quarter. He was therefore respected by the men for more reasons than one and, when he shouted for them to be silent, they promptly obeyed and settled down to listen to the Head Shed.

'Can I just open,' Captain Callaghan asked rhetorically, 'by saying that I know how frustrated you men have been, stuck here in Gloucestershire, when the battle for Europe is under way in France.'

'Damned right, boss!' Lance-Corporal Jack 'Jacko' Dempster cried out. 'The best bloody brigade in the British Army and they leave us sitting here on our arses while lesser men do all the fighting. A right bunch of prats, that's how we feel.'

As the rest of the men burst into laughter or murmurs of agreement, Sergeant Lorrimer snapped: 'We don't need your bloody nonsense at this time in the morning, Jacko. Just shut up and let the boss speak or I'll have you out in a guard box.'

'Yes, Sarge!' the lance-corporal replied with a smirk.

Nevertheless, Lorrimer was grinning too, for he had a great deal of respect for Dempster and the rest of the 'other ranks'. Jacko, as everyone knew him, was just one of the many men in the room who had been founder members of

L Detachment when it came into existence in 1941. Known as the 'Originals', they included Sergeants Bob Tappman, Pat Riley and Ernie Bond; Corporals Jim Almonds, 'Benny' Bennett, Richard 'Rich' Burgess and Reg Seekings; and former Privates, now Lance-Corporals, Neil Moffatt, Harry 'Harry-boy' Turnball and, of course, Jacko Dempster.

Each one of these men had gone into the North African desert with minimal knowledge of desert warfare, learnt all there was to know from the Long Range Desert Group, and then taken part in daring, mostly successful, raids against Axis airfields located well behind enemy lines. Remarkably, only one of them – the revered Lieutenant John 'Jock' Steel Lewes – had died during those raids. As a brutal climax to the final raid of that period – a simultaneous attack by three different groups against Sirte, Tamit and Nofilia – the survivors, all now present in the briefing room, had made it back to the forward operating base after an epic trek across the desert, most of them practically crawling into their camp at Jalo Oasis. Though they never openly said so, they were proud of what they had accomplished and stuck together because of it, keeping themselves slightly apart from the other, more recent arrivals in the SAS Brigade.

Furthermore, as Sergeant Lorrimer knew only too well, the Originals had developed a low boredom threshold, and this had caused immense frustration when, at the end of 1943,1 SAS were returned to Scotland for training and operations in northern Europe. Initially they were kept busy establishing a base near the remote village of Darvel, east of Kilmarnock; but in May the following year the SAS Brigade had been moved to Fairford, where the men had been able to do little more than constant retraining in preparation for Operation Overlord. Small wonder they had become even more frustrated when D-Day passed without them. Now Lorrimer was hoping that what the CO was about to tell them would make amends for that.

'Well, gentlemen,' Captain Callaghan continued, 'to end the suspense, we've been assigned a specific task in France and it commences forthwith.'

When the cheering, clapping and whistling had died down, the captain continued: 'At this moment, General Patton's 3rd Army is driving south towards Dijon.'

'Mad Dog Patton!' shouted Corporal Richard 'Rich' Burgess.

'I wouldn't let him hear you say that, Corporal,' Callaghan admonished him, 'because although he may seem mad to you, he's a damned good soldier and proud of it.'

'Sorry, boss.'

'Anyway, to aid Patton's advance, Montgomery has asked for airborne landings in the Orléans Gap.'

'That's us?' Lance-Corporal Harry 'Harry-boy' Turnball asked hopefully.

'No,' Callaghan replied. '*Our* task is to soften up the enemy before the landings – and to distract them from the landings – by engaging in a series of hit-and-run raids against their positions. For this mission, Operation Kipling, you and your jeeps will be inserted by parachute in central France. Once you've all been landed, you'll establish a base, lie low and make contact with the Maquis.'

'Frogs?' Lance-Corporal Neil Moffatt asked dubiously.

'French partisans,' Captain Callaghan corrected him. '"*Maquis*" is a Corsican word meaning "scrub" or "bush". The Maquis are so called because when the Krauts introduced compulsory labour in the occupied countries, many men fled their homes to live in rudimentary camps in the scrubland and forests. Since then, with the aid of our Special Operations

Executive and America's Office of Strategic Studies, they've been engaged in highly successful sabotage activities behind German lines. They may be Frogs to you, but they're a bunch of tough, courageous Frogs, so don't knock them.'

'Sorry, boss,' Neil mumbled.

'Good or not, why do we need 'em?' Rich Burgess asked.

'Because we believe their local knowledge will make them invaluable for planning raids, particularly those behind enemy lines.'

'Are they troublesome?' Sergeant Bob Tappman asked.

Callaghan nodded. 'Unfortunately, yes, and for a couple of reasons.'

'Which are?'

'The Maquis are split between those who support General de Gaulle's Free French and those who sympathize with the communists. Unfortunately, the latter believe, as do the communists, that de Gaulle is no more than Britain and America's stooge, to be used and then discarded.'

'Bloody marvellous!' Corporal Reg Seekings murmured, then asked: 'Anything else?'

'Yes,' Callaghan said. 'A lot of the Maquis have shown more interest in storing weapons for after the war, to use against de Gaulle's supporters, than they've shown in actually killing Germans.'

'Beautiful!' Jacko said, laughing. 'I can't wait to work with them.'

'Also,' Callaghan pressed on, 'the SOE views the Maquis as its own concern, has its own teams to arm and organize them, and therefore won't take kindly to us becoming involved. In fact, they've already unofficially voiced their complaints about the plan to insert us in what they view as their own territory.'

'Well, stuff the SOE!' Rich exploded.

'I agree,' said Bob Tappman. 'Those sods don't know anything about the real world. We can deal with the Maquis better than they can, so let's go in and get on with it.'

'Nevertheless,' Callaghan continued, 'even given these negative points, we *do* believe that with the advent of D-Day and the continuing advance into Europe, the Maquis will be more co-operative than they've been in the past. They'll want the war to end as soon as possible . . .'

'So that they can get stuck into each other,' Jacko interrupted, copping a laugh from the other men.

'. . . to enable them to sort out their differences,' Callaghan continued, ignoring the interjection. 'We're banking on that.'

'And what if it doesn't work out that way?' Bob Tappman asked bluntly.

Callaghan nodded to Greaves, then stepped aside to let his fellow captain take centre stage. 'Where we're going,' Greaves explained, 'the situation is changing constantly, so our own position there will be highly unpredictable. Therefore we have to be ready to change our plans at a moment's notice. What I'm about to outline to you is a preliminary course of action that'll be subject to changing circumstances on the ground.'

'I love surprises,' said Jacko.

'I should point out, first thing,' Greaves continued, 'that we won't be alone. The Special Air Service Brigade, consisting of British, French and Belgian components, was flown into France shortly after D-Day and has since set up a wide network of bases in Brittany, the Châtillon Forest, east of Auxerre, the area around Poitiers and the Vosges. Some of these groups are working hand in glove with the Maquis; others are out there on their own. Either way, they were inserted in order to recce the areas, receive stores, and engage in active operations only after our arrival.'

'So when and where do we arrive?' Bob Tappman asked.

In response, Greaves picked up a pointer and tugged the canvas covering off the blackboard, to reveal a map drawn in white chalk and showing the area of central France bounded by Orléans to the west, Vesoul to the east, Paris to the north and Dijon to the south. 'We'll parachute in here,' he said, tapping a marked area between Rennes and Orléans, 'and then make our way by jeep through the forest paths north of Orléans. The vehicles will be dropped by parachute once you men have landed. They're modified American Willys jeeps equipped, as they were in North Africa, with twin Vickers K guns front and rear, supplemented with 0.5-inch Browning heavy machine-guns. The modified versions have a top speed of approximately 60mph and a range of 280 miles, though this can be extended by adding extra fuel tanks, so you should get anywhere you want to go with a minimum of problems.'

'And where do we want to go?' Jacko asked.

'With the recent American breakthrough at Avranches, we've been presented with a fluid front through which small vehicles can pass. The American Advance Party already has one troop spread across a direct line from Normandy to Belfort, roughly across the centre of France. With those men already in place, and with ensured air supply for our columns, we're in a good position to cause chaos behind the Germans who're withdrawing in front of the US 3rd Army led by General Patton. Therefore, in order to lend support to Patton's advance and help his 3rd Army reach Dijon, you men will head initially for the Châtillon Forest and, once there, make contact with the Maquis. You will then learn everything you can about the area from the Maquis and, using that knowledge, embark on a series of hit-and-run raids, preferably by night, against enemy positions.'

'How far do we take the raids, boss?' Bob Tappman asked in his customary thoughtful manner.

'Nothing too daring, Sergeant,' Greaves replied. 'Nothing too risky. The point is to harass them – not engage in unnecessary or lengthy fire-fights – and to sabotage their channels of communication and, where possible, destroy their transport. The task is harassment and distraction, rather than elimination – so just get in and out as quickly as possible. And no heroics, please.'

'You won't get any heroics from us, boss,' Jacko said, lying for all of them. 'No one here wants a bullet up his arse if he can possibly avoid it. We all want to live to a ripe old age.'

In fact, Jacko was not alone in thinking that the last good time he had had was a month ago, when on a weekend pass to London. After the peace and quiet of Gloucestershire, he and the other Originals had been thrilled to find the West End so lively, with staff cars and troop carriers rumbling up and down the streets, Allied bombers constantly roaring overhead, protected by Spitfires and other fighter planes, flying to and from France; the pavements thronged with men and women in the uniforms of many nations; the parks, though surrounded by anti-aircraft guns, packed with picnicking servicemen and civilians; ARP wardens inspecting the ruins of bombed buildings while firemen put out the latest fires; and pubs, cafés, cinemas and theatres, albeit with black-out curtains across the windows and their doorways protected behind sandbags, packed with people bent on enjoying themselves.

Even during the night, when diminishing numbers of German bombers flew over to pound London and V-l and V-2 flying bombs caused further devastation, the city was packed with soldiers, pilots, sailors and their women, all having a good time despite the wailing air-raid sirens, exploding bombs, whining doodlebugs, blazing buildings and racing ambulances. Compared with tranquil Gloucestershire, the capital was a hive of romance and excitement, for all the horrors of war. In truth, it was where most of the Originals wanted to be – either on leave in London or taking part in the liberation of Europe. The latter was, at least, now happening and they would soon be part of it. That made Jacko, and most of the others, feel much better. They were back in business at last.

'What's the transport situation?' Sergeant Pat Riley asked.

'Handley-Page Halifax heavy bombers specially modified to carry men and supplies and drop jeeps and trailers from its bomb bay,' said Greaves.

'Bloody sitting ducks,' Neil Moffatt whispered to his mate, Harry 'Harry-boy' Turnball.

'Not any more,' the captain said to Neil, having overheard his whispered remark. 'In fact, the Halifaxes are now armed with two .303-inch Browning machine-guns in the nose turret, four in the tail turret, and two in manual beam positions, so we should have adequate protection should we be attacked by enemy fighters during the flight.'

'Thanks, boss, for that reassurance,' Neil said wryly.

'Is it true, as some of us have heard, that we're having problems in getting enough aircraft?' Rich Burgess asked.

'Unfortunately, yes. Because we don't yet have our own planes, all arrangements for aerial transport have to be co-ordinated by 1st Airborne Corps and 38 Group RAF at Netheravon and Special Forces HQ. This means that we practically have to bid for aircraft and we don't always get enough for our requirements. For this reason, you should expect to be inserted in batches over two or three successive nights; likewise for the jeeps.'

'Which means that those who go earliest have the longest, most dangerous wait on the ground,' Rich said. 'More sitting ducks, in fact.'

'Correct,' Greaves replied with a grin. 'Which means in turn that the most experienced men – including you, Corporal – will be in the first aircraft off the ground.'

'Gee, thanks, boss,' Jacko said, imitating an American accent with no great deal of skill.

'Do we take off from Netheravon?' Bob Tappman asked.

'No. From RAF Station 1090, Down Ampney, not far from here. Station 1090 will also be giving us support throughout our period in France.'

'So when do we get out of here,' Rich asked, 'and get to where it's all happening?'

Greaves simply glanced enquiringly at the CO, Captain Callaghan, who stepped forward to say: 'Tomorrow night. You'll be kitted out in the morning, collect and manually test your weapons throughout the afternoon, and embark at 2250 hours, to insert in central France just before midnight. Any final questions?'

As the response was no more than a lot of shaking heads, Callaghan wrapped up the briefing and sent the men back to their barracks with instructions to pack as much as they could before lights out. They needed no encouragement.

2

Next morning the men rolled off their steel-framed beds at first light, raced to the toilets, then had a speedy cold shower and shaved. Cleaned and jolted awake by the icy water, they dressed in Denison smock, dispatch rider's breeches and tough motor-cycle boots. The smock's 1937-pattern webbing pouches held a compass and ammunition for the .455-inch Webley pistol, which was holstered at the hip. Though most of the newer men wore the paratrooper's maroon beret with the SAS's winged-dagger badge, as ordered by a directive of the airborne forces, of which they were presently considered part, the Originals viewed the directive as an insult and were still defiantly wearing their old beige berets.

Once dressed, they 'blacked up' their faces and hands with burnt cork, which they would keep on all day and at least throughout the first night in France. They then left the barracks and crossed the parade ground to the mess hall at the far side, most glancing up just before entering the building to see the many Fortresses, Liberators and escorting Spitfires flying overhead on their way to France for the first of the day's bombing runs. In the mess, which was filled with long, crowded tables, steam, cigarette smoke and a lot of noisy conversation, they had a substantial breakfast of cereal, bacon, fried eggs and baked beans, with buttered toast or fried bread, and hot tea.

'The last day we're going to get decent grub for a long time,' Jacko said to the men at his table, 'so enjoy it, lads. Only two more to go.'

They tucked in as best they could in the time allocated to them, which wasn't much; then, with full bellies, they left the mess hall and walked briskly to the armoury, where they collected their personal and other weapons. These were, apart from the Webley pistol, which they already had, of a wide variety, most chosen by the individual for purely personal reasons and including 9mm Sten sub-machine-guns, Thompson M1 sub-machine-guns, more widely known as 'tommy-guns', and Bren light machine-guns. Their criss-crossed webbing was festooned with thirty and thirty-two-round box magazines, hand-grenades, a Fairburn Sykes commando knife, a bayonet, binoculars and some Lewes bombs – the latter invented by the late Lieutenant John 'Jock' Steel Lewes and first used in the North African desert in 1941.

Burdened down with their weapons, they scrambled into Bedford QL four-wheel-drive trucks and were driven to a firing range at the southern end of the camp. There, as the sun climbed in the sky and the summer heat grew ever stronger, they lay in the dirt and took turns at firing their various weapons, simultaneously practising their aim and checking that the weapons worked perfectly and did not jam. After a couple of hours, they stripped and cleaned the weapons, slung them over their shoulders, then clambered back into the trucks and were driven back to their barracks. There they deposited their weapons in the lockers by their beds before returning to the mess hall for lunch.

'The second-to-last decent meal for a long time,' Jacko reminded his mates, 'so tuck in, lads.'

After lunch they were marched to the quartermaster's store, where they picked up their bergen rucksacks, groundsheets, survival kit, including water bottles, first-aid box, tin mug and plates with eating utensils, and finally their Irvin X-Type parachute. Another hour and a half was spent packing the kit into the rucksacks and checking thoroughly that the chute was in working order, then they strapped the rucksacks, rolled groundsheets and parachute packs neatly to their backs, picked up their weapons and left the barracks like beasts of burden.

'All right, you ugly mugs,' Sergeant Lorrimer growled at the men, standing before them with his clenched fists on his broad hips, as bombers rumbled overhead on their way to France, 'get in a proper line.'

After being lined up and inspected by their respected sergeant, who had an eagle eye and a sharp tongue when it came to error and inefficiency, they were marched to the waiting Bedford trucks, clambered up into them, and were driven out of the base and along country roads to Down Ampney and RAF Station 1090. On the way they passed columns of troop trucks heading away from many other staging areas and bound for various disembarkation points along the coast, where the boats would take them to France to join the Allied forces already there. Above, the cloudy sky was filled with Allied bombers and fighter escorts likewise bound for France. Such sights gave most of the men a surge of excitement that had been missing too long, and eased the bitter disappointment they had been feeling at missing D-Day.

'Nice to know we're joining them at last,' Rich said to his mate Jacko. 'We've been stuck here too long.'

'Bloody right,' Jacko replied, waving at the troops heading in the opposite direction in Bedfords. 'And we'll be there in no time.'

After passing through the heavily guarded main gates of the RAF station, they were driven straight to the airfield, which was lined with both British and American bombers, as well as the fighters that usually escorted them to Germany. Disembarking from the trucks at the edge of the airfield, near a modified Halifax bomber being prepared for flight and the Willys jeeps waiting to be loaded on to it, they were greeted by Captains Callaghan and Greaves.

'How goes it, boss?' Sergeant Lorrimer asked Callaghan.

'Not too well,' Greaves replied bluntly. 'Captain Callaghan and I have wasted most of the day desperately phoning between 1st Airborne Corps and 38 Group RAF at Netheravon and Special Forces Unit, begging for more aircraft for the drop.'

'Bloody waste of time,' Callaghan said curtly to Sergeant Lorrimer and the other ranks grouped around him. 'By the time we'd finished we still had only one Halifax to go with – this one here.'

'Which means,' Greaves cut in, 'that we will, as feared, have to insert the men and jeeps over two or three nights.'

'Wonderful!' Lorrimer murmured sardonically. 'What a bloody waste of time!'

Callaghan nodded wearily, then continued: 'Since then, we've been rushing around trying to finalize routes, supplies and men, and liaise with the units across the water. Everything's now set for the drop, but the insertion will necessarily be tedious. The most experienced men will therefore go first.'

'That's us,' Jacko said.

'Lucky us,' Rich added. 'We'll be on the ground with Krauts all around us and we won't be able to do a sodding thing until the others are dropped. Two or three days of high risk coupled with boredom – a fitting reward for experience.'

'Stop whining,' Lorrimer told him. 'When it's over you'll be boasting about it in every pub in the land. You should *thank* us for this.'

'Gee, thanks, Sarge!' Rich replied.

'All joking aside,' Callaghan said, 'this business of not having our own aircraft means we're practically having to beg for planes that are constantly being allocated elsewhere at the last moment, leaving us strapped. I don't like being at the mercy of 1st Airborne Corps or 38 Group RAF. Sooner or later, we'll have to get our own air support – always there when we want it.'

'I agree,' Greaves said. 'But in the meantime we'll have to live with our single Halifax.'

'All right, let's get to it.'

Already well trained for this specific task, the Originals of C Squadron, who would go on the first flight, removed the twin Vickers K guns normally mounted to the front and rear of the modified American Willys jeeps, along with the 0.5-inch Browning heavy machine-guns, and placed them in separate wooden crates. Then, with the aid of short crates and nets operated by REME, the jeeps were placed in their own crates, which had air bags underneath to cushion the impact on landing. When the lids had been nailed down, four parachute packs were attached to each crate. To facilitate the drop, the aircraft's rear-bay doors had already been removed and a long beam fastened inside, so the men rigged each crated jeep with a complicated arrangement of crash pans and struts, then attached it to the beam to spread the load.

'Those should slow your darling down a bit,' Jacko said to the RAF pilot standing beside him, referring to the crated jeeps and weapons.

The pilot, who was chewing gum, nodded. 'They'll certainly have an adverse effect on the aircraft's performance, but apart from making it sluggish to fly, there should be no great problems.'

'Unless we're attacked by Kraut fighters.'

'Hopefully they'll take care of that,' the pilot said, pointing at the other RAF men who had already entered the Halifax and were taking their positions behind the two .303-inch Brownings in the nose turret and the four in the tail turret. The remaining two guns in the manual beam positions would be handled in an emergency by one of the other seven crew members. 'They'll make up for our sluggishness,' the pilot added.

'Let's hope so,' said Jacko.

By the time the last of the crates had been fixed to the beam in the rear bay, darkness was falling. Once the rest of the RAF crew had taken up their positions in the aircraft and were checking their instruments, the men of C Squadron were ordered to pick up their kit and board the Halifax through the door in the side. After forming a long line, they filed in one by one and sat side by side in the cramped, gloomy space between the fuselage and the supply crates stowed along the middle of the dimly lit hold. Shortly after, the RAF loadmaster slammed the door shut and the four Rolls-Royce Merlin 1390-hp, liquid-cooled engines roared into life, quickly gained power, and gradually propelled the Halifax along the runway and into the air.

Flying at a speed of just over 685mph, the aircraft was soon over the English Channel, though the SAS men in the windowless hold could not see it. All they could see directly in front of them were the wooden supply crates which, though firmly strapped down, shook visibly each time the aircraft rose or fell. Glancing left or right, all that each trooper could see were the profiles of the other men seated along the hold, faces pale and slightly unreal in the weak yellow glow of the overhead lights.

The hold was long, too crowded, horribly noisy and claustrophobic, making many of the men feel uncomfortable, even helpless. This feeling was in no way eased when, over France, the Halifax was attacked by German fighters and the Brownings front and rear roared into action, turning the din in the hold into absolute bedlam. To make matters worse, the Halifax began to buck and dip, obviously attempting to evade the German Stukas, and the piled crates began banging noisily into one another while making disturbing creaking sounds.

'Christ!' Neil shouted, to make himself heard above the noise. 'Those bloody crates are going to break away from their moorings!'

'If they do, they'll fall right on top of us,' his friend Harry-boy Turnball replied, 'and crush more than our balls. They'll bloody flatten us, mate!'

'Or crash right through the fuselage,' Jacko put in, 'and leave a great big fucking hole that would see us sucked out and swept away. Put paid to the lot of us, that would.'

Even above the clamour of the Halifax's engine and the banging, groaning supply crates, they could hear the whine of the attacking Stukas and the deafening roar of the Brownings.

Suddenly, there was a mighty explosion outside the Halifax, which shuddered from the impact, followed by cheering from the front of the plane. The RAF sergeant acting as dispatcher, standing near the crated jeeps in the bomb bay, gave the thumbs up.

'They must have knocked out one of those Kraut fighters,' Rich said. 'I just wish I could see it.'

'Right,' Jacko replied. 'Bloody frustrating being stuck in here while all that's going on outside. Makes a man feel helpless. I'd rather be down there on the ground, seeing what's going on.'

'Too right,' Rich agreed.

In fact, they didn't have long to wait. The buzz of the Stukas faded away, the Brownings ceased firing, and the Halifax, which had been dipping and shaking, settled back into normal, steady flight. Ten minutes later, it banked towards the drop zone (DZ) and the dispatcher opened the door near the bomb bay, letting the angry wind rush in.

'Five minutes to zero hour,' he informed the men, shouting above the combined roar of the aircraft's engines and the incoming wind, which beat brutally at the seated men. 'On your feet, lads.'

Standing up, the SAS paratroopers fixed their static lines to the designated strong points in the fuselage and then waited until the dispatcher had checked the connections. This check was particularly important as the static lines were designed to jerk open the 'chutes as each man fell clear of the aircraft. If the static line was not fixed properly to the fuselage, it would slip free, the canopy would not open and the unlucky paratrooper would plunge to his death. A man's life could therefore depend on whether or not his static line was secure.

Satisfied that the clips would hold firm, the dispatcher went to the open door, leaned into the roaring wind, looked down at the nocturnal fields of France, hardly visible in the darkness, then indicated that the paratroopers should line up, ready to jump. As they were already in line, having been seated along the length of the fuselage, they merely turned towards the open door, where the wind was blasting in, and stood there patiently, each man's eyes focused on the back of the head of the soldier in front of him.

Because he could not be heard above the roar of wind and engines, the dispatcher mouthed the words 'Get ready!' and pointed to the light-bulb above his head. Looking up at the light, which would signal the start of the drop, the men automatically tried to become more comfortable with their harnesses, moving the straps this way and that, checking and rechecking their weapons, then doing the same with their equipment.

'Close your eyes and think of England,' Rich murmured, though most of the others merely took very deep breaths and let it out slowly, each coping with the rush of adrenalin in his own way.

The light turned to red. Two minutes to go.

As CO, Captain Callaghan was back at base, waiting to come out with the third and last group, and Captain Greaves was heading Group One. Greaves therefore took up a position beside the open door, from where he could check that each man had gone out properly before he became the last man out. The first man to jump was Sergeant Lorrimer, not only because he was the senior NCO, but because he was going to act as 'drifter', indicating the strength and direction of the wind.

Taking his place by the open doorway in the fuselage, Lorrimer braced himself, leaned into the beating wind, took a deep breath and looked down at what appeared to be a bottomless pit of roaring darkness. Eventually the dispatcher slapped him on the shoulder and bawled: 'Go!'

Lorrimer threw himself out.

First swept sideways in the slipstream, he then dropped vertically for a brief, deafening moment. But suddenly he was jerked back up when the shoot was 'popped' by the fully extended static line secured inside the aircraft. Tugged hard under the armpits, as if by the hands of an unseen giant, he then found himself dropping again, this time more gently, as the parachute billowed open above him like a huge white umbrella.

In just under a minute the seemingly infinite darkness beneath him gained shape and definition, revealing the moon-streaked canopy of the dense forest north of Orléans. No sooner had Lorrimer glimpsed this than the trees were rushing up at him with ever-increasing speed. Tugging the straps of the parachute this way and that, he steered for the broad, open field that was now clearly visible and watched the trees slip away out of view as he headed for the DZ. The flat field seemed to race up to meet him and he braced himself for contact. The instant his feet touched the ground, he let his legs bend and his body relax, collapsing to the ground and rolling over once to minimize the impact. The whipping parachute dragged him along a few feet, then collapsed, and he was able to snap the straps free and climb to his feet, breathless but exhilarated.

Glancing about him, he saw no movement either in the dark expanse of field or in the forest surrounding it. Relieved that he had not been spotted by the Germans, who were doubtless in the vicinity, he looked up at the sky and saw the blossoming white parachutes of the rest of the men, most of whom were now out of the Halifax.

Having carefully observed Lorrimer's fall and gauged from it the wind's strength and direction, the pilot had banked the Halifax to come in over an area that would enable the paratroopers to drop more easily into the field, rather than into the forest. Now, they were doing so: first gliding down gently, then seeming to pick up speed as they approached the ground, hitting it and rolling over as Lorrimer had done, then snapping the straps to set themselves free from the wildly flapping parachute.

Having disengaged himself, each man used the small spade on his webbing to quickly dig a small hole in the earth. Then he rolled up his chute and buried it. This done, he unslung his assault rifle and knelt in the firing position, all the while keeping his eyes on the trees. By the time the last man had fallen, the paratroopers were spread out across the field in a large, defensive circle, waiting for the Halifax to turn around and drop the crates containing the jeeps and supplies.

This did not take long. The aircraft merely turned in a wide circle above the forest, then flew back to the field. When it was directly above the DZ, the crates were pushed out of the open rear bay and floated down, each supported by four parachutes. The. men in the field had to be careful not to be standing under a crate when it fell, even though its landing was cushioned by the air bags beneath it.

Soon those not on guard, keeping their eyes on the surrounding forest, were using their special tools to split the crates open and get at the jeeps. Once out of the smaller crates, the twin Vickers K guns and the 0.5-inch Browning heavy machine-guns were remounted on the Willys jeeps and the vehicles were then driven into the forest and camouflaged. When the field had been cleared, the wood from the packing crates was buried near the edge of the trees and the upturned soil covered with loose leaves.

'Now let's get into hiding,' Greaves told his men, 'and wait for the others to be dropped tomorrow night.'

'*And* the next night,' Lorrimer said in disgust.

The men melted silently into the edge of the forest flanking the DZ, taking up hidden positions near the field's four sides. There, they proceeded to make individual lying-up positions, or LUPs, by scraping small hollows out of the earth, covering them with wire, and laying local vegetation on top. Having eaten a supper of cold rations washed down with water, the men bedded down for the night, most of them in their LUPs, others taking turns at guard duty. Placed in the four directions of the compass on each side of the field, the lookouts scanned the forest for any sign of the enemy.

There were no land movements apparent that night, though many aircraft, both Allied and German, flew overhead to engage in bombing runs or aerial fights far away. While the surrounding forest was quiet, the sounds of distant explosions were heard all night as battle was engaged on several fronts and the Allied advance across France continued. When dawn broke, the mist of the horizon was smudged with clouds of ugly black smoke.

'Poor bastards,' Jacko murmured, thinking of the unfortunate men who had endured the relentless bombing all night near that murky horizon.

'Poor *Kraut* bastards,' Rich said ironically.

'A lot of them are Allied troops,' Jacko reminded him, 'being bombed by the Germans. But whatever side they're on, they're poor bastards, all of them. I don't like bombardments.'

'I grant you that, mate. We had enough of them in North Africa and Sicily to last us a lifetime. I'm amazed we've still got our hearing as well as our balls.'

'Some would dispute the latter assertion,' Sergeant Lorrimer whispered as loudly as he dared, raising his head from the LUP beside them. 'Now shut up, fill your mouths with some cold food, then go and replace those poor frozen sods out on point.'

'Yes, Sarge!' Jacko and Rich whispered simultaneously.

For most of the men, the rest of the day was long and boring, with nothing for them to do but either lie in their LUPs or crawl out to replace one of the guards. Aircraft, mostly

Allied, flew overhead constantly, Fortresses and Liberators and accompanying Spitfire fighters, intent on keeping up the relentless bombing of German positions further inland.

Also, throughout the day, German convoys or individual jeeps and trucks could be seen passing by on the nearby road, half obscured by the hedgerows that bounded the fields, heading towards or away from the front indicated by the distant sounds of battle. Luckily, none of them turned off the road to cross the field to the forest and the SAS men remained undetected.

When darkness fell, the sounds of distant battle were accompanied by spectacular flashes that lit up the horizon and lent a magical glow to the dense clouds. Shortly before midnight, the Halifax reappeared overhead and the white parachutes of the second batch of SAS men billowed in the darkness as they drifted gently to earth. They were followed by another consignment of wooden crates, each one descending beneath four parachutes and landing on their air bags.

When the aircraft had disappeared again, the new men did exactly as the first batch had done: drove their jeeps into the forest, buried the wooden planking from the crates and covered the disturbed earth with leaves, then scraped out LUPs in areas selected for them by the Originals, who had landed the previous night.

Another night passed uneventfully, except for distant explosions from the front and eerie flashes which lit up the horizon, revealing swirling clouds of smoke. The smoky dawn heralded a second tedious day, with Allied aircraft rumbling almost constantly overhead and helmeted German troops heading to and from the front on the road beyond the field, at the other side of the hedgerows. Hidden in their LUPs, the men were not seen by the German troops, though some were already so bored that they wished they had been.

That night the third and last of the SAS groups, headed by Captain Callaghan, was brought in to the DZ by the Halifax. This time, however, one of the jeeps dropped from the aircraft broke free from two of its four parachutes and crashed to the ground, causing the crate to shatter and the waiting soldiers to run for cover. The jeep had embedded itself so deeply in the ground that it had created a large crater. Because the vehicle was badly damaged, it was left buried there, along with all the other debris, and then the hole was filled in with soil and camouflaged with loose foliage.

This time, instead of melting back into the trees, the new arrivals helped the first two batches of men to fill in their LUPs and hide all trace of their presence in the area. Then the men of C Squadron, now safely on the ground, dispersed to their individual jeeps and the column, totalling twenty vehicles, moved off along a forest track, heading for the open country behind enemy lines.

3

Aided by bright moonlight, which illuminated the narrow road through the forest, the column of jeeps had a relatively easy first morning, heading without lights for open country dotted with small farming communities. Some of the villages, as the men knew, were still occupied by the Germans and so had to be approached carefully; others had been freed but were surrounded by the advancing and retreating armies, which meant that the Germans could return unexpectedly; and an increasing number were well out of the danger zone and preparing to give a heart-felt welcome to their Allied liberators.

Progress was frustratingly slow because one jeep was out ahead on point, its crew having been given the dangerous job of acting as advance scouts, prepared to either engage the enemy or, if possible, return unseen to the main column and report the enemy's presence to Captains Callaghan and Greaves, who would then jointly decide if they should attack or simply make a detour. The brief, as outlined by Callaghan, was to avoid engaging the enemy whenever possible and instead reconnoitre the area for a suitable base camp from where they could move out to find the Maquis.

In fact, more than once the men on point in the jeep – Sergeant Lorrimer as driver, Jacko on the twin Vickers K guns and Rich on the Browning heavy machine-gun – noticed the glow of camp-fires and oil lamps in the forest and assumed them to be from German camps. Invariably, closer inspection, usually on foot, revealed this to be true and the men therefore always had to backtrack to meet up with the column behind and inform Callaghan and Greaves of the enemy presence. The column, now split into two, with Callaghan in charge of Group One and Greaves leading Group Two, would then take the nearest side road and make a wide detour around the enemy, to travel on unmolested.

This was the situation for most of the first six hours, as they travelled through the night and early morning in the depths of the forest. By dawn, however, the trees were thinning out and they were emerging into open countryside with wide, rolling fields dotted with hamlets and crossed by a web of major and minor roads, including German military supply routes (MSRs).

'It looks so peaceful out there,' Callaghan said.

'Except for that smoke on the horizon,' Greaves replied. 'It's all happening there.'

Now out in the open, they had to travel much more carefully. To get from one side of an MSR to the other, they usually drove alongside it, out of sight behind hedgerows or trees, until they came to where the road was crossed by a track. There they would wait until the track was inspected by the jeep on point; when it was reported clear, the column of jeeps, using the track, would cross at top speed. Once or twice the last of their jeeps crossed just as retreating German columns appeared along the MSR and headed towards them; but that first day, at least, they managed to push on unseen.

The first village they came to was on the banks of the Loire. Arriving there just before noon, they were greeted by villagers, mostly women, children and elderly men who cheered, applauded and placed garlands of flowers around the soldiers' necks. The soldiers then learned that they were the first Allied troops to arrive; that the Germans had only recently fled from this village; that three of the villages around it were still occupied by sizeable German columns; and that the Germans were reported to have recently fled from the next village along the SAS men's route.

As most of the soldiers settled down in the sunny village square to flirt with the bolder local girls while enjoying a lunch of fresh bread, cheese and calvados, all supplied by the grateful villagers, Callaghan and Greaves received a visit from the mayor and the sole remaining member of the Maquis. The mayor was a portly, good-humoured individual who gave them invaluable information about the German forces who had occupied the village. The Maquisard was a young man, Pierre, who wore shabby grey trousers, a torn tweed jacket, shoes with holes in the soles and a rakishly positioned black beret. With a stolen German semi-automatic rifle slung over his shoulder, he grinned cockily as he told them, in French, that the rest of his Maquis friends had left the village in pursuit of the fleeing Germans and that he had been left behind to act as guide to the first Allied troops to arrive.

'That means us,' Callaghan said.

'*Oui, mon capitaine*. I will be proud to serve.'

'Ah, you speak English!'

Pierre grinned and placed his index finger just above his thumb, leaving a tiny gap between them. 'Only a little.' Then, reverting to his own language, he said: 'But your French, I notice, is excellent.'

'It's good enough,' Callaghan said, though he spoke the language well, 'I'm sure we'll get by with it. What was it like with the Germans here?'

Pierre shrugged and stopped grinning. 'Not good, *monsieur*, but other villages had it worse. Here, though the Boche commandeered the best houses and took most of the food we grew, they were a disciplined bunch who neither harmed the older folk nor abused the women. They *did* take the few remaining young men away for forced labour in Germany, but as most of us knew they would do that when they came, we fled into the forest and made our own camps there.'

'And were very successful at harassing the Germans,' Greaves said diplomatically.

'In a limited way only – at least until the invasion was launched. Before that, we had to be careful about coming out of the forest to attack the Germans, because if we did they would exact some terrible form of vengeance. Sometimes they shot three or four Frenchmen for every German shot by us, or even worse, in one case they herded every member of a village into the church and then set fire to it. So some of them have done terrible things, but here we were lucky.'

'And your fellow Maquisards are now pursuing those same Germans?'

'Sniping on them as they retreat. The main German supply route, along which they are retreating, runs through hilly, densely forested countryside. The Maquis are well protected by the trees and pick them off from the hills. This not only reduces the Germans in number, but also makes them constantly nervous. I wish I was there!'

'You can be,' Callaghan told him. 'It's imperative that we link up with the Maquis and learn all we can about the

Germans' movements and habits. If you act as our guide, you'll be able to rejoin your companions.'

'Then I'm your man, *mon capitaine*.'

'Thank you, *monsieur*.'

Callaghan glanced across the village square and saw that the SAS troopers not on guard at the edge of the forest encircling the village were sprawled around the fountain in the middle of the square, in the shade of the leafy trees, finishing off their bread and cheese, swigging calvados, and shamelessly flirting with the younger, bolder girls. The girls' parents were looking on, not offended, simply thrilled to see the British soldiers here, scarcely believing that they were human like other men, and might seduce their daughters. The fountain itself, Callaghan noticed, had been hit by a bomb and was now half demolished and covered with its own rubble and pulverized cement. There was no sign of water.

'When do we move out?' the young Maquisard asked, removing his semi-automatic weapon from his shoulder and laying it across his thighs, where he lovingly stroked it.

'When we've checked that the next village has been cleared, I want you to go with a forward patrol, lead them to the village, see what's happening, then return here. If we know that the village is cleared, we can move on to link up with the Maquis.'

'Very good,' Pierre said.

Nodding at Sergeant Lorrimer, who was kneeling beside the young Frenchman, Callaghan asked: 'Do you mind doing this?'

'My pleasure,' Lorrimer replied. 'That calvados perked me up no end and now I'm raring to go.'

'Then take Pierre with you and try to get back here as soon as possible. Be careful, Sergeant.'

'I will, boss,' Lorrimer said. 'OK, Pierre, come with me.' When Pierre stared uncomprehendingly at him, Lorrimer stood up and jerked his thumb, indicating that the Frenchman should follow him. With Pierre beside him, he walked around the smashed fountain to where Jacko and Rich were sitting on the steps of a house, enjoying themselves by trying to communicate with two giggling girls who spoke almost no English.

'No, you don't understand,' Jacko was saying, indicating himself and the dark-haired girl nearest to him by jabbing at her and himself with his index finger. 'Me . . . love . . . you. Me want to get in your knickers.'

The girl, not understanding what he was saying, started giggling again, though Rich silenced her by saying: 'That's bloody rude, Jacko! They're decent girls.'

'And we're their conquering heroes, so we might as well . . .'

'Shut your filthy mouth, Jacko,' Lorrimer growled as he approached the men, 'and get to your feet. Before you cause offence here by saying the wrong thing in front of a Frog who knows English, I'm taking you on a little patrol.'

'Aw, come on, Sarge!' Jacko protested, wiping his wet lips with the back of his hand and waving his bottle of apple brandy. 'I haven't finished my lunch!'

'You've had enough for now. And if you have any more of that stuff you'll be even more stupid and loose-tongued than you are normally. So put that bottle down, pick up your rifle, and get on your feet. You, too, Burgess.'

'Very good, Sarge,' Rich said, slinging his rifle over his shoulder and winking at the moon-eyed French girl beside him. 'Unlike some we could mention, I never complain about being asked to perform my duty. Backbone of the squadron, me, Sarge.'

'And humble with it, I note,' Lorrimer responded. 'Now say goodbye to your two little girlfriends and let's get to the jeep.'

Rich shyly mumbled his farewell to the girl sitting beside him, but Jacko, climbing to his feet, was considerably more theatrical, bowing, sweeping his beret across his chest and saying with a dreadful accent: '*Au revoir, mademoiselle. Je t'adore.*' When the girl burst into giggles again, Jacko grinned from ear to ear, then followed Lorrimer, Rich and the young Maquisard across the square to their jeep.

'I didn't know you spoke French,' Rich said.

'I don't,' Jacko replied. 'Those are the only Frog words I know. Picked them up from the films.'

'What a fucking prat!' Sergeant Lorrimer muttered to himself, shaking his head in exaggerated disgust. Then, indicating the young Frenchman with the German rifle, he said: 'This is Pierre, of the Maquis. If you understand what I'm saying, Pierre, this is Corporal Burgess, known as Rich, and Lance-Corporal Dempster, known as Jacko. As neither speaks French, you won't have to put up with their bloody awful conversation.'

'Well, thanks a lot!' Jacko exclaimed.

'I understand,' Pierre said proudly, smiling at everyone. 'Rich and Jacko! Nicked names!'

'Nicked names,' Lorrimer said. 'You've got it.' He sighed in exasperation and turned to the other two. 'Pierre's going to act as our guide and hopefully lead us to his fellow Maquis. But first he'll take us to the next village on our route. If it's been cleared, which we think it has, we'll come back and tell the others about it. Then we head out.'

'You picked the right men for the job,' Jacko informed him.

'I'm sure,' Lorrimer said, then he clambered up into the driver's seat of the Willys jeep, indicated that Pierre should sit beside him, and waited patiently until Jacko and Rich had climbed into the back, the former behind the twin Vickers guns mounted in the middle of the vehicle, between the front and rear seats, the latter behind the Browning heavy machine-gun mounted on the rear. 'All set?' Lorrimer asked.

'Of course,' Jacko replied.

'Fire away,' Rich added.

'Hold on,' Lorrimer said. Just to take the wind out of the sails of his two cocky passengers, he released the handbrake and accelerated quickly, making the tyres screech in the soil as the jeep shot forward, practically taking wing. Jacko and Rich were nearly thrown out and had to hold on to their mounted machine-guns to stay upright; they were still frantically trying to keep their balance when their SAS mates in the square, still eating and drinking, clapped their hands and cheered, before being obscured in the cloud of dust churned up by the departing jeep.

'Mad bastards!' Callaghan muttered as he watched the jeep disappear around the first bend in the track, heading into the forest.

'Lorrimer's just having some sport,' Greaves replied, grinning. 'They'll be all right.'

In the jeep, as Lorrimer slowed it down to a less suicidal speed, Jacko spread his legs and continued to steady himself by holding on to the grips of the twin Vickers. 'Very good, Sarge!' he bawled above the roaring of the vehicle. 'A real smooth getaway!'

'Designed to wake you up,' Lorrimer replied. 'And clearly it did.'

'Bloody right,' Rich confirmed, likewise holding on tight to his machine-gun.

'Very quick! Most admirable!' Pierre added, trying out his English. 'We will be there in no time. Take this track, *s'il vous plaît*.'

Following the direction indicated by the Frenchman, Lorrimer turned off the main road and took the narrower track heading east, winding through dense, gloomy forest. The narrowness of the track and its many bends, and the overhanging branches of trees, slowed him down considerably, but he would have gone slower anyway to enable Jacko and Rich to thoroughly scan the forest for any sign of German snipers. In this task Pierre was even more of a help, knowing the forest intimately, but no movement was evident among the dense trees.

Ten minutes later they were, Pierre loudly informed them, approaching the next village.

'Slow down when I signal,' he managed to say in a mixture of French, English and sign language. 'Stop, please, when I tell you.'

Lorrimer slowed down and stopped entirely when Pierre, at a bend in the narrow track around which they could not see, dropped his right hand with the palm face down. When Pierre indicated that they were going to walk the rest of the way to the village, Lorrimer executed a difficult turn on the narrow track, so that the jeep was facing back the way it had come. Having cut the engine and applied the handbrake, he picked up his 9mm Sten sub-machine-gun and jumped to the ground.

'You, too,' he said to Pierre, then turned to Jacko and Rich to say, as Pierre jumped down beside him: 'You two keep manning those guns. If you hear us running back – or hear or see anything else indicating that we're being pursued by Jerry – get ready to open fire. Understood?'

'Yes, Sarge,' both men replied, simultaneously swinging their machine-guns around on their swivel mounts until the barrels were facing the track at the rear of the jeep.

'Good. Let's go, Pierre.'

Lorrimer and the Maquisard walked away from the jeeps and turned the bend in the track, both with their weapons unslung and at the ready. At the other side of the bend, the track ran straight to the tiny village, and gave a partial view of the sides of several stone cottages with red-slate roofs. The village, Lorrimer noted, was only about five hundred yards away and smoke was coming out of the chimneys.

Using sign language, he indicated that he and Pierre should leave the track and advance the rest of the way through the trees. This they did, encountering no one and soon emerging near the backs of the cottages.

From the open window of one of the cottages, they could hear a crackling radio on which someone was speaking in French. Though not familiar with the language, Lorrimer understood enough to realize that he was hearing news of the Allied liberation of the country. The advance seemed to be going well.

Stepping up to the house and glancing through the open window, Lorrimer saw that the kitchen was filled with people, all seated around a huge pine table, drinking wine or calvados, smoking cigarettes and. listening with obvious pleasure to the news on the radio. That they were doing so was a clear indication that the Germans had already left.

Sighing with relief, but still not taking any chances, Lorrimer checked the rear of the other cottages in the row, and found similar scenes inside, so he let Pierre lead him out into the village's only street.

The street was no more than a flattened earth track running between two straight rows of stone cottages and a grocer's, animal feed store and saddlery, bakery, dairy, blacksmith's, barber's shop, one bar and, at the far end, a church, graveyard and school. Many of the locals – mainly farmers and their wives, most surprisingly plump and red-cheeked given the spartan existence they must have led during the German occupation – were sitting either on their doorsteps or on rush chairs outside the houses, taking in the sun, eating and, like those Lorrimer had seen in the kitchens, celebrating with wine or calvados.

When those nearest to Lorrimer and Pierre saw them, they came rushing up excitedly to embrace them, kiss them on both cheeks or shake their hands, and then plied them with bread, cheese, alcohol, all the while asking about the Allies' progress. After refusing the wine and telling them as much as he knew, Lorrimer asked if all the Germans had left the village.

'They left two behind as snipers,' he was informed in English by a solemn-faced, gaunt man wearing an FFI armband. 'But they didn't last long.' Straightening his shoulders and grinning, he turned away to point along the street. Looking in that direction, Lorrimer saw two German troopers sprawled on their backs in the dirt, their helmets missing – probably taken as souvenirs – and their heads a mess of blood and exposed bone where they had been shot. The FFI man patted the pistol strapped to his waist and smiled again at Lorrimer. 'Me,' he said proudly. 'I killed both of them. There are no more Boche here.'

'Good,' Lorrimer said. 'We intend bringing our men through here, so please send someone back to warn us if any Germans return.'

'Naturally,' the man said, clearly relishing his role as protector of the hamlet.

Lorrimer thanked the man and walked back along the village street, with Pierre beside him. 'A good man,' Pierre said. 'He hates the Germans. And those who fraternize.' They were passing a crowd that had gathered around the barber's shop and walked over to see what was happening. An attractive young woman of no more than twenty was having her head shaved by the village barber while the excited crowd, mostly women and children, looked on, laughing and occasionally spitting at the weeping woman. 'She slept with a German soldier,' Pierre explained, smiling brightly at Lorrimer. 'A collaborator bitch.'

'Probably just in love,' Lorrimer said, turning away in disgust.

Pierre shrugged. 'In love . . . a whore . . . whatever – she still collaborated. That's all we care about here.'

'Let's get back,' Lorrimer said.

They returned via the narrow, winding forest track to the jeep, where Jacko and Rich were keeping the bend covered in silence.

'The village has been cleared,' Lorrimer told them, 'so let's get back to the squadron.'

'They must have heard you coming,' Jacko said.

'And got scared shitless,' Rich added.

'Any more fancy remarks and you'll be *walking* back,' Lorrimer said as he climbed into the driver's seat and turned on the ignition.

'These lips are sealed,' Jacko said.

'Same here, Sarge,' Rich added.

'Glad to hear it, lads,' said the sergeant, waiting until Pierre was sitting in the seat beside him before releasing the handbrake and heading back to the first village.

Twenty minutes later they emerged from the gloomy forest and drove into the centre of the sunlit village, where Lorrimer told Jacko and Rich to remain in the jeep until he had reported to Callaghan and Greaves. The two captains were sitting in the shade of a tree near the remains of the fountain, studying a map.

Though disgruntled at being prevented from again fraternizing with the pretty village girls, Jacko and Rich received some consolation when they hurried up to the jeep, gave them more bread, cheese and wine and began flirting with them. Shaking his head in mock exasperation, but unable to conceal a grin, Lorrimer ignored them while he crossed to the square, accompanied by Pierre, and knelt in the dirt beside Callaghan and Greaves.

'The next village has been cleared,' he informed the officers. 'The only Germans still there are the two dead ones lying in the street.'

'The FFI took care of them?' Callaghan asked shrewdly.

'Yes, boss.'

'Where would we be without our French patriots? Right, Sergeant, let's get doing.'

The column of jeeps moved out shortly after, churning up great clouds of dust that descended on the men, women and children in the square, most of whom waved goodbye and threw flowers over the departing vehicles. Once back on the forest track, amid the now familiar gloom and silence, the men manning the guns in the jeeps carefully scanned the trees on both sides, on the lookout for snipers. In the event, nothing happened and soon they were rounding the last bend in the track and emerging on to the sunlit road that ran straight through the village.

The SAS men responded with understandable pleasure to the women and children who ran alongside their vehicles, throwing flowers and handing up more bottles of calvados. Their spirits, however, were momentarily dampened when they passed the woman who had had her head shaved and now, completely bald and streaked with blood, was kneeling in the dirt, covering her face with her hands and trembling as she sobbed. Thankfully, they were soon past her and circling around the two dead German troopers spread-eagled in the middle of the road; then they were leaving the village behind and heading out into open country again.

In the dimming light of the late afternoon, they could still see the smoke on the horizon, where battles were raging along the constantly shifting front. Throughout the journey they saw no German troops, though Luftwaffe planes occasionally passed overhead, mainly bombers escorted by Me-109 fighters, heading for England and some desperate, last-minute air raids. How these aircraft managed to get as far as Britain was a mystery to most of the SAS men, since the sky above them seemed to be filled constantly with Allied aircraft flying in from Britain and recently recaptured Normandy airfields to bomb German positions in front of the advancing Allied troops.

'They must just ignore one another,' Rich suggested, 'because the missions they're on are more important. Just fly right past each other.'

'I s'pose so,' Jacko replied. 'No sense in it otherwise.'

Later in the evening, as the sun dimmed and huge shadows crossed the rolling green and brown hills, the smoke on the horizon was illuminated by the silvery flashes of countless explosions. It was not a welcoming sight.

'We'd better find somewhere to stay for the night,' Callaghan said. 'I think we've travelled far enough from the DZ and the men could do with a break.'

'I agree,' said Greaves.

They picked the next isolated farmhouse they came to. Not wishing to act like the Germans and commandeer the farmhouse itself, they decided to make simple LUPs on the unused field directly behind it. Nevertheless, when Callaghan and Greaves climbed down from their respective jeeps and knocked on the door of the farmhouse, the farmer refused to come out. Frustrated, the short-tempered Callaghan forgot his manners and blew the lock off the door with his Webley. He then kicked the door open and strode in, followed closely by Greaves.

Inside, in a living-room smelling of dry rot and filled with crying cats, saucers brimming with milk and cat food, strung-up dead rabbits, and ancient rustic furniture, they found the French farmer and his wife cringing behind a moth-eaten sofa and tentatively raising their hands above their heads.

Exasperated, Callaghan spoke to them in French, explaining that he and his men were English and merely wished to camp for one night at the back of the farm and have access to water and the outdoor toilet. All cooking, he explained, would be done by his men on their own portable stoves. Even so, because the farmer had been under the yoke of the Germans for years, the proposal terrified him.

'But what if the Germans return and learn that I've helped you?' he asked, his voice shaking. 'They would shoot me!'

'Then let them bloody well shoot you!' the increasingly irate Callaghan exploded in English, unable to reconcile the difference between this trembling wretch and the warmly welcoming French people in the last two villages they had past through. 'If they don't shoot you, I will!' he added in French. 'We're staying! You understand?'

'*Oui, monsieur*!' the shocked Frenchman snapped.

'Damn it, we're here to help you!'

'*Oui, monsieur*!' the farmer's wife said quickly.

'You have a pump round the back?'

'*Oui, bien sûr*.'

'Good. We'll use it for our water. We'll use your outdoor toilet and ensure that it doesn't get blocked. We'll do our cooking on our own stoves and ensure that the leftovers and rubbish are buried in the field. We'll leave no mess. Your house will not be entered. When we leave tomorrow, you'll hardly know we've been here. Is that acceptable to you?'

'Of course, *monsieur!*' the farmer said. 'Naturally, Captain!'

'Good,' Callaghan repeated. 'We'll do all this on the grounds that you don't leave your farm and tell no one, French or German, that we're here. Should you do so – or should you, in any other way, give us trouble – I personally will put a bullet through your thick head. Is that understood?'

'Yes, *monsieur!*' the farmer replied, practically babbling.

'Then good night to you, sir.'

Flushed with anger, Callaghan turned away from the cringing farmer and his wife, and, followed by Captain Greaves, went to the back of the house to organize his sixty men, most of whom were now sitting or stretched out on the field by their parked jeeps.

As they were only staying for one night, and as tents could more easily be seen by a passing enemy, Callaghan told the men to make LUPs similar to those they had used at the DZ when first inserted on French soil. As they had done before, the men merely scraped small hollows out of the earth, covered them with wire and spread foliage on top. Since they had not had a hot meal since their arrival in France – though they were certainly grateful for the bread, cheese, wine and calvados generously proffered by the grateful locals – they were given permission to use their hexamine stoves for simple fry-ups and making tea.

A couple of hours later, when the food had been consumed, each trooper doused the flames of his still-burning hexamine blocks, cleaned his stove and put it back in his bergen rucksack. He then queued up for as long as forty minutes to use the outdoor toilet, before gratefully lying down in his LUP for a fitful sleep punctuated by the sound of explosions from the distant front, accompanied by spectacular, silvery flashes illuminating the dark horizon where soldiers, British and German alike, were dying all through the night.

Nevertheless, they managed to rise at first light from their LUPs, if not exactly full of the joys of spring, at least sufficiently rested to face the new day.

4

Passing through more scattered villages from which the Germans had fled, the SAS column naturally attracted the attention of the locals, who plied the men with food, alcohol and information about enemy troop movements. Unfortunately, in many cases they were more enthusiastic than accurate and while much of the information was valuable, a lot of it had to be discarded after causing great confusion, such as sending the SAS men off in the wrong direction, sometimes practically right into enemy hands, sometimes into areas being bombed or shelled by the Allies. Nevertheless, while this led to some hair-raising experiences, by nightfall the column had travelled another fifty miles, or a third of its planned journey, and Captain Callaghan was well satisfied.

By now Callaghan had learnt that because of the constant Allied bombing, the Germans were mostly moving under cover of darkness. Therefore he decided that his own men would move during the day and rest in LUPs during the night. He also decided that it would be safer to divide into three smaller columns, spaced approximately thirty minutes apart, to ensure that the whole squadron could not be attacked at once. He placed himself in charge of the first column of seven jeeps,

Captain Greaves in charge of the second, also seven jeeps, and Sergeant Lorrimer in charge of the third, consisting of the remaining six jeeps. It was the latter who had the first encounter with the enemy.

The three columns had been advancing all morning and into the early afternoon, ever deeper behind enemy lines, guided by the excitable Maquisard Pierre, now in Callaghan's jeep, and always keeping well away from the smoke-wreathed horizon where the main battles were raging along a broad front. The squadron had divided earlier that morning, with the second two columns moving out at thirty-minute intervals after the first and fanning out in opposite directions. Every two hours, however, they circled back to meet at prearranged RVs, where they would rest, eat cold rations and trade information about what they had seen and heard, before parting again.

Soon after emerging from the darkness of the Forêt de Dracy and *en route* to the next RV, which was near Avallon, Lorrimer, following Callaghan's Group One and well in front of Greaves's Group Two, found his way blocked by a broad river.

'Shit!' he hissed, then checked his map and looked up at Jacko and Rich. 'The River Yonne,' he informed them. 'It runs south, right past Avallon, which is on the east bank. We've got to get to the other side, so let's follow it downstream until we find a bridge.'

'You're the driver, Sarge,' Jacko said chirpily from behind the twin Vickers guns. 'Ours is to obey.'

'I should bloody well hope so,' Lorrimer said, rising once again to the bait. He stood behind the steering wheel and used a hand signal to indicate that the five other jeeps should follow him, and then sat down again, engaged the gears and led the column south, following the muddy track alongside and above the river.

The jeeps bounced roughly along the track for a distance that should have taken them half an hour but actually took almost three because they got bogged down again and again, with the jeeps' noses tipped forward and the front axles buried deep in the mud. When this happened, the men, groaning with frustration, rescued the vehicles with a variation on a system first devised in the deserts of North Africa. First they unloaded the heavy kit and weapons to lighten the jeep; then, after scraping or digging away the mud from the trapped wheels, they placed modified five-foot-long steel sand channels under them. When these were firmly in place, the jeep, with its engine running in low gear, could be pushed forward on to a succession of further channels until it was back on firm ground.

It was sweaty, exhausting, filthy work that left the men caked in hardening mud, but it had to be done.

'Bloody awful,' Lance-Corporal Neil Moffatt complained, kneeling on the river bank and trying to rub the mud from his face and hands with a wet cloth, which only seemed to spread it even more. 'I hate this filthy business. It was bad in the heat of the fucking desert, but at least it was sand, not this stinking mud. I could scream doing this.'

'Right,' said his mate, Harry 'Harry-boy' Turnball, who was kneeling beside him and also trying to clean himself. 'And Christ knows what slimy bastards are crawling about in this mud, itching to give us some filthy disease. I *hate* this bloody stuff!'

'The only disease you're going to get,' Corporal Reg Seekings told him, 'is the clap from some poxy French tart.'

'He should be so lucky,' Jacko told them, standing behind them and looking on, amused, smoking. 'The way they responded to him in the villages we've already passed through, I'd say he'd be lucky even getting himself a hag. A dead dog's about all he'd get near – and even that might be shocked back to life and run away at the sight of him.'

'Very funny,' Harry-boy said. 'I'm splitting my sides here.'

'All right, you men, you're filthier than you were before,' Lorrimer bawled at them. 'Let's waste no more time. Get back in the jeeps.'

The journey along the river bank continued, with the jeeps continuing to get stuck in mud every few minutes. Eventually, however, they came to a bridge linking two MSRs. About a hundred yards wide, it was constructed from wooden planks lashed together, but was strong enough to support heavy vehicles.

Stopping at the bridge, Lorrimer carefully scanned the far bank for signs of enemy troops, but saw no sign of movement in the murk of the dense forest.

'What do you think?' he asked Jacko and Rich.

'Impossible to say,' Jacko replied. 'The only way we'll find out if Jerry's covering that bridge is to drive across it.'

'As fast as we can,' Rich added thoughtfully.

'All right, let's do it,' Lorrimer said. 'Hang on to your berets, lads.'

After letting the jeep bounce down on to the planks, Lorrimer accelerated and started to race across. The bridge shook dramatically as the other jeeps thumped down on to it one after the other; the tyres made the planks rumble like jungle drums and the wind, whipping at the exposed men, followed the course of the river with a loud, rushing sound.

Lorrimer was about halfway across when a machine-gun roared on the far bank. Instantly, a hail of bullets ricocheted noisily off the struts of the bridge just above the jeep.

Jacko and Rich returned fire with their machine-guns, sweeping left to right in a broad arc that tore branches and leaves off the trees along the opposite bank. Unable to see where the enemy fire was coming from, they just hammered away in a sweeping motion as bullets ricocheted around them and the jeep raced towards the relative safety of the bank. They stopped firing when the jeep practically flew off the bridge at the far side, smashing through the overhanging foliage and racing along the track into the forest.

As Lorrimer put his foot on the brake, Jacko and Rich clung once again to their machine-guns, using them for balance. Glancing back, they saw the next two jeeps following each other off the bridge, bouncing dangerously as they did so. However, the tyres of the third exploded when it was peppered with German bullets and it slewed left as it bounced off the track and crashed into a tree trunk.

Accurately judging where the gunfire was coming from, Jacko opened fire with his .303-inch twin Vickers, squinting grimly along the sight, which was located between the two round-shaped 250-round belt feeds, firing in long, savage bursts, and turning the forest to his left into a storm of flying leaves and branches. Rich followed suit, raking broadly from left to right, the combined guns making that part of the forest look like it was being torn apart by a tornado.

A man's scream rang out above the harsh rattling of the machine-guns and the German fire stopped abruptly. This enabled the men in the damaged jeep – Sergeant Tappman and Lance-Corporals Moffatt and Turnball – to jump out and run for the shelter of the nearest trees. As they were doing so, the second two jeeps screeched to a halt close to Lorrimer's and the last two bounced off the bridge and managed to get into the shelter of the trees before the German Spandau machine-gun started up again.

'I don't bloody believe this!' Jacko yelled, then raked the

same area, tearing the trees to shreds and this time making the Germans stop firing.

'Get in there!' Lorrimer bawled to the men who had escaped from the damaged jeep and were frantically unslinging their assault rifles. 'Finish off those bastards!'

Tappman and the two lance-corporals instantly raced towards the area devastated by the machine-guns of Jacko and Rich. Spreading out, crouched low, their weapons at the ready, they disappeared into the undergrowth. Seconds later, their combined 9mm Sten sub-machine-guns and Thompson M1 sub-machine-guns roared in short, savage bursts. Then there was silence.

When the three men reappeared, Tappman stuck his thumb in the air, indicating that the remaining Germans had been dealt with.

'A single machine-gun crew?' Lorrimer asked when the men had returned to his jeep.

'Yes, Sarge, just one. Four men, one machine-gun.'

'What about your jeep?'

'All the tyres have been blown out and the petrol tank's shot to buggery. We can kiss it goodbye.'

'Any of you men hurt?'

'Not a scratch.'

'Lucky you,' Lorrimer said dispassionately. 'So, since you're still alive, strip everything out of that fucked jeep and spread it around the other vehicles. Then each of you can take the spare seat in one of the others.'

When the spare kit and weapons had been removed from the abandoned jeep and distributed around the squadron, the three men took spare seats and the column moved off again, winding through the dark forest until they emerged on the edge of another village deserted by the Germans. As they drove along the single street, the villagers swarmed excitedly around them, cheering, shouting greetings in French and offering the customary bread, cheese and wine.

One of them, who had an idiot's grin, clambered on to the bonnet of Lorrimer's jeep to rant in a mixture of French and pidgin English about how he would help the SAS kill more of the Boche. When he refused to get down, Lorrimer removed his Webley from its holster and tapped the barrel against the man's forehead.

'Off the jeep,' he said firmly.

The man's eyes widened and turned, almost crossing, to focus on the barrel of the pistol, then he grinned, slipped to the ground and disappeared back into the crowd.

As the others closed in on the jeep, offering greetings and gifts, an attractive, dark-haired woman in her mid twenties, wearing muddy dungarees and flushed with excitement, said in English: 'God, I can't believe it! You're actually here at last!'

Stunned to recognize a West Country accent, Sergeant Lorrimer asked: 'Are you English?'

'Yes,' the young woman replied. 'Anne Gardner.'

'What on earth are you doing here?'

Smiling as if slightly embarrassed, the woman glanced at the villagers packed tightly around her and now listening in as best they could without knowing the language. 'Oh, I married a Frenchman I met in St Austell, where I lived with my family before the war. I was only eighteen then. He was a farmer and he brought me back here. I've lived here ever since.'

'You were here when the Germans occupied the village?'

'Yes.'

'How did they treat you?'

'No different from the others, thank the Lord. I always spoke French and they never asked to see my papers – only my husband's. Then they took him away.' When tears started from her eyes, she quickly wiped them away. 'Forced labour in Germany.'

'He's there still?'

'I presume so.'

'I'm sorry.'

The sound of laughter and shouting made Lorrimer glance over his shoulder. Directly behind him, in the jeep, Jacko and Rich were still at their machine-guns, though Jacko was leaning down to take a bottle of calvados from one of the women. 'No more drinking!' Lorrimer bawled. 'Give them back the bottles. And pass the word along the column.'

'Aw, come on, Sarge, just . . .'

'*Give it back!*' roared Lorrimer.

Hearing the tone of the sergeant's voice, Jacko shrugged and rolled his eyes at the woman with the bottle, indicating that he could not accept it.

'Sooner or later we'll be confronted by more Germans,' Lorrimer explained, 'and I don't want you men pissed when that happens. So pass the word down the line: no more drinking today.'

'Right, Sarge, will do.'

Still holding the grips of his twin Vickers, Jacko turned away to shout Lorrimer's order along the column. As the expected moans and groans arose from the other jeeps, Lorrimer, ignoring them, turned back to the Englishwoman.

'We were ambushed by a lone bunch of Germans when we crossed the river back there,' he told her. 'Are there any more that you know of still around?'

The woman nodded and pointed her finger. 'Back there,' she said, 'is a whole regiment – about a hundred men in all.'

Seeing that she was pointing south, where the other two SAS columns were exploring, though thirty minutes apart,

Lorrimer decided that he had better check the area and, if necessary, mount a rescue operation if one or other of the columns, led by Callaghan and Greaves, had got into trouble.

'Would you show me where the Germans are?' he asked.

'Of course,' the Englishwoman said. 'I'll take you most of the way. Then you can drop me off and I'll walk back. I can't fire a gun.'

'I'm very glad to hear *that*,' Lorrimer said, grinning, charmed by the young woman's manner. 'Take the seat beside me.'

When the woman had climbed up beside him, Lorrimer drove off, following her directions. Within five minutes they had passed through more thick forest and eventually emerged to where the road suddenly snaked around the top of a steep cliff and back down again. At the bend, the woman told Lorrimer to stop the jeep.

'They were just around that bend,' she said. 'At the base of the cliff. You should see them if you get out and walk along, using the ditch at the side of the road for cover.'

'You'd make a good soldier,' Lorrimer told her, jumping down from the jeep as the woman did the same the other side. 'Thank you and goodbye.'

'Good luck,' the woman replied, then, after waving to Jacko and Rich, she hurried back along the road and disappeared around the first bend. Unslinging his 9mm Sten gun, Lorrimer said to the two men: 'I'm going around that bend alone, but keep your eyes peeled and your ears unblocked.'

'We're right behind you,' Jacko said.

'That's what I'm afraid of,' Lorrimer replied. 'I don't want my arse shot off.'

He walked to the side of the road and slithered down into the ditch that ran alongside it. The ditch was narrow and, being filled with stones, was awkward to walk along, but he made his way carefully around the corner with only his head visible above the rim.

That was enough. The instant he rounded the bend, the roar of a Spandau machine-gun split the silence and bullets ricocheted noisily off the lip of the ditch, sending pieces of stone and earth raining down, cutting his face and temporarily blinding him.

Ducking low, but then carefully raising his head again, Lorrimer caught a glimpse of the Germans. Their jeeps, armoured cars, tanks and horse-drawn gun carriages were resting under the trees by the road below, obviously hoping to ambush passing Allied troops. Having kept in contact with Groups One and Two by means of the No. 11 wireless set in the radio jeep, he knew that if they had not already done so, both groups would be returning along that same road just before sunset, heading back to the RV. If either group did so, it would be ambushed.

'Damn!' Lorrimer murmured.

Judging by the number of vehicles visible through the trees, there were certainly a lot of Germans – probably a hundred or so, as the girl had suggested – and they were clearly well armed.

The team firing the Spandau had spotted Lorrimer's head from the back of their horse-drawn gun carriage. Even now, their spotter, just about visible through the overhanging branches, was scanning the upper road with binoculars, only lowering them when he wanted to indicate a new line of fire by jabbing his finger in Lorrimer's direction. The bullets continued to tear up the lip of the ditch, coming closer to him each second.

Satisfied with what he had seen, Lorrimer began making his way back, but before he reached the bend again the other jeeps raced towards him, with Rich driving the lead vehicle and Jacko already firing bursts from his twin Vickers. The guns of the other jeeps roared into action as the vehicles rounded the bend, strafing the German positions below and temporarily silencing the machine-gun that had been trying in vain to find Lorrimer.

Glancing back over his shoulder, Lorrimer saw that the forest all around the German vehicles was being torn to shreds by the hail of bullets from the machine-guns mounted on the SAS jeeps. Even so, the German troops were well protected in their armoured cars and behind their truck, and clearly something more forceful was required.

Even as Lorrimer was deciding that a few mortar shells might do the tricks, the German machine-gunner started firing again and the ground along the rim of the ditch spat soil and stones, encouraging Lorrimer to hurry back along the ditch until he came abreast of his jeep, still in the lead. The column was placed near the far side of the track, which gave it a certain degree of cover behind the lip of the ditch, but the top half of the vehicles, from where the men were firing, was exposed to enemy gunfire.

'I want a couple of mortars in that ditch,' Lorrimer bawled at Jacko, 'to put out that Spandau and damage some of their armoured vehicles. Pass the word down the column.'

Jacko shouted Lorrimer's instructions to the jeep directly behind him and Corporal Jim Almonds, heading that vehicle, shouted the instructions on to the men in charge of the group's two 3-inch mortars.

As the fire from the Spandau was joined by that of other machine-guns, showering the SAS troops in earth and vegetation from the overhanging trees, the two mortar teams clambered out of their jeeps and hurried as fast as they could across the road to the ditch, burdened as they were by their heavy equipment, including the mortars and steel base plates. Once in the relative shelter of the ditch – where they were nevertheless constantly showered by soil and stones – they expertly bedded the base plates by packing them in with some of their smoke bombs.

In one team, Corporal 'Benny' Bennett, one of the Originals from the war in the North African desert in 1941, was directing the firing, which was done by Neil Moffatt. In the second team, Harry-boy Turnball was directing and Reg Seekings firing.

The first shells used were smoke bombs – selected not only to cause discomfort to the Germans, but also to provide a visual aid for the two men directing the fire. The mortars roared and their shells exploded in the forest about 200 yards beyond the German positions.

Using the rising columns of smoke as markers, Bennett and Turnball gave new instructions to the two gunners, who fired two more smoke bombs at a much sharper angle. This time, the smoke billowed up darkly from close behind the last German armoured car visible through the trees. Knowing that a slightly sharper angle of fire would land the shells directly on target, Benny and Harry-boy gave revised instructions and were gratified to see the resultant columns of smoke billowing up from between the enemy's armoured vehicles.

Satisfied, they instructed the gunners to replace the smoke bombs with 4.54kg high-explosive shells, which erupted with a mighty roar, tearing the trees to shreds and setting fire to some of the branches. When the first two HE shells were followed by another two, the combination of smoke, fire and flying debris forced the Germans to flee in all directions, some of them running out into the road. There, they were cut down by a savage fusillade from the SAS machine-guns, semi-automatic weapons and assault rifles.

Deciding to risk the mortar explosions rather than the withering hail of SAS fire, the surviving German troops rushed back into the blazing, smoking forest, leaving their many dead and wounded on the road behind them. Within minutes Lorrimer and his men had the satisfaction of seeing the undamaged German vehicles pulling out of the trees and tearing off along the road, weaving to avoid the exploding mortar shells and continuing gunfire. When they were out of sight, with only the dead and wounded still on the road or in the forest, Lorrimer hand-signalled 'Cease fire' and a startling silence descended.

'Tell the signaller to get on the radio,' the sergeant said, 'and inform Captain Callaghan that the route to the RV has been cleared.'

'Will do, Sarge,' Jacko replied, releasing the grips of his Vickers and vaulting over the side of the jeep.

'And get confirmation that we can all proceed to the RV straight away,' added Lorrimer.

'Got you, Sarge.'

'And while you're at it, check if we have any casualties.'

'Anything else, Sarge, before I leave?'

'That'll do for now, Jacko.'

'I am on my way, Sarge.'

Lighting up a Senior Service and puffing a cloud of smoke, Jacko hurried back along the column to have words with the signaller in the radio jeep. While Jacko was away, Lorrimer and Rich both lit up Players and puffed away with great pleasure while gazing down at the dead and wounded Germans on the road. As there was little sign of movement down there, the wounded had to be few in number.

'We'll have to pick them up,' Lorrimer said thoughtfully.

'Why?' Rich asked in his quiet, oddly dispassionate manner.

'Can't just leave 'em there to die,' Lorrimer replied. 'Too slow. Too painful. They could freeze to death tonight or even get eaten by wolves.'

'So be it,' Rich said. 'What would we do with them, Sarge? They'd just be a bloody nuisance.'

'Certainly bloody,' Lorrimer replied, surveying the dead and wounded. 'But we can't leave them there. If we meet up with the others at the RV, where we'll also join up with the Maquis, we can load those poor bastards on trucks and drive back to the nearest field hospital.'

'Those poor bastards were trying to kill us,' Rich said, exhaling a cloud of cigarette smoke.

'We were trying to kill them,' Lorrimer answered, 'so I reckon we're even now.'

Jacko sauntered back with the cigarette still smouldering between his lips. Clambering up into the jeep, he said: 'No, we have no casualties. Yes, we can proceed directly to the RV.' He took up his position behind his Vickers, then continued: 'Group One is at the RV already, having managed to get past that stretch of road down there before Jerry arrived. We're to take off now and Group Two, which is about thirty minutes south of here, will follow in about thirty minutes. Captain Callaghan said to thank us for clearing the road for him. He would have copped it otherwise.'

'That he would,' Lorrimer said. 'A right little massacre.' He raised his right hand, then brought it down in a cutting motion, indicating that the column should move out after his jeep. Taking his seat behind the steering wheel, he turned on the ignition and set off, following the road as it curved sharply left and dropped steeply, until the column reached the dead and wounded Germans far below the cliff top. There, Lorrimer demanded that two men get out of each jeep to drag the German dead to the side of the road and hump the wounded into the SAS jeeps. This they did with a great deal of grumbling, many of them agreeing with Rich that the enemy wounded could become a nuisance, others wanting to put a bullet through their heads and be done with it. Eventually, however, the route was cleared, the German dead heaped up around the trees by the side of the road and their four wounded stretched out on the rear seats of the jeeps, one man to each vehicle.

'Right,' Lorrimer said, squinting into the setting sun, 'let's get to the RV.'

As the sun sank and the shadows lengthened, they found themselves driving into hilly, densely forested country around the Forêt de St Jean, where, they knew, the Maquis were in hiding. Darkness had just about fallen when, following the grid references on their maps, they approached the RV. Guided in by Morse code flashed on lamps held by fellow SAS troops on the hills, eventually they found themselves driving into a huge, uncompleted laager formed by Groups One and Two in a clearing surrounded by protective hills and forest.

Only when their own column was parked, completing the laager, and when the four wounded Germans had been placed temporarily on camp-beds in the hospital tent, were the men of Group Three allowed to climb down and join the other men sitting in clusters near their camouflaged bell tents, cooking hot food and boiling tea over open fires or on hexamine stoves.

As the Maquisard Pierre told Lorrimer when the sergeant reported to Captain Callaghan, the bell tents actually belonged to the men of the Maquis, most of whom were presently patrolling the hills and would not be back until first light. The SAS men had been allowed to light fires and use their portable stoves because only Allied aircraft were flying over this area and the laager itself was well guarded by troopers taking four-hour stints on watch.

Exhausted by their long, eventful journey, the men of Group Three enjoyed a hot meal, then unrolled their sleeping bags and stretched out around the bell tents, under the stars, to catch up on some badly needed sleep.

5

As the gentle shafts of first light fell on the bell tents of the Maquis and the laager of SAS vehicles, some of the men woke to see figures emerging spectrally from the mist that still wreathed the trees of the thickly wooded hills. Unshaven, dressed in baggy grey or black trousers, black boots or heavy shoes, and drab, faded jackets, and with peaked caps on their heads, they might have been taken for farmworkers were it not for the bandoliers of ammunition criss-crossing their bodies, the hand-grenades hanging from their belts and the mixture of British, American and German weapons they were holding at the ready.

If this surprised the watching SAS men, many of whom were still sitting up in their LUPs and rubbing the sleep from their eyes, they were even more surprised to see that some of the shabbily dressed men were in fact women.

'I think I must be dreaming,' Callaghan said to Greaves as the two slipped out of the sleeping bags laid down in the shallow LUPs they had diplomatically decided to dig near those of their NCOs and troopers.

'Some of them are pretty as well,' Greaves replied, 'as you can see when you get a good look at their faces.'

'Not so easy under all that dirt – and not so easy to see their bodies beneath those baggy clothes. But, yes, some of those girls *are* attractive!'

Indeed, one of the consolations of this war, Callaghan was thinking as he stood up and adjusted his uniform, having slept in it, was that the squadron was moving through a land populated with ordinary people – not just fellow troopers, enemy soldiers, or male Arabs and camels, as it had been in the North African desert back in '41. Here, particularly in the liberated villages, they had seen many women, young and old. Clearly, some of them had decided to do their bit with the Maquis and were, as he noted when they drew closer, mostly young and pretty, albeit smeared with the dirt used as camouflage.

He and Greaves were distracted from their instinctive study of the womenfolk when a lean, handsome, unusually intense man, about thirty years old, stepped out from the group and stopped right in front of them.

'Ah!' he exclaimed softly but sardonically. 'The English have arrived at last!'

'Yes,' Callaghan replied.

'British Army?'

'Yes. The Special Air Service, 1st Airborne Division.'

'Ah, yes, the SAS! I have heard much about you.' The man adjusted his M1 carbine on his left shoulder and held out his right hand. 'André Flaubert, leader of the local Maquis.'

Callaghan shook his hand. 'Captain Patrick Callaghan, Commanding Officer of C Squadron. And this is Captain Derek Greaves, my second in command.'

'Pleased to meet you,' Greaves said formally, shaking the Frenchman's hand.

André Flaubert nodded toward the sleeping bags. 'You slept there?'

'Yes.'

'As Commanding Officer and second in command you should have better than that.'

'As the men were sleeping like that last night, I thought we should do the same. We'll fix up better accommodation when the tents arrive with the resup planned for tonight.'

'Resup?'

'Further supplies. Dropped by parachute.'

'Ah, yes, I see.' Nodding, not smiling, the Maquis leader glanced back over his shoulder to see the rest of his group, men and women, dispersing to their individual tents. Then he looked back at Callaghan and Greaves. 'Come,' he said. 'We can talk in my tent. Have you had breakfast yet?'

'No.'

'Then we can talk while we eat.'

The SAS men, apart from those on guard duty, were already splashing cold water on their faces or lighting their hexamine stoves, to make breakfast, as the officers accompanied André to his tent. It was only slightly bigger than the others, though big enough to contain not only the usual camp-bed, but also a trestle-table, a blackboard with maps of the local area draped over it, and at least three wooden chairs for guests. A portable wood-burning stove had been set up on a table just outside the tent and one of the dirt-smeared Resistance women was heating coffee on it while filling bread rolls with cheese and tomato.

'Please,' André said with a distracted wave of his hand, taking the chair at the far side of the trestle-table, just in front of the blackboard. 'Take a seat.'

Callaghan and Greaves each took one of the wooden chairs at the other side of the table, feeling as if they were being interviewed in someone's office. The woman outside, hardly more than twenty and already an experienced fighter by the look of her, had prepared the food and was pouring the coffee into four tin mugs.

'How long have you led this group of Maquisards?' Callaghan asked, to get the conversation rolling.

'Four years,' André replied, still not smiling. 'Since the Germans first came to the village. We knew they were on the way and also knew, from the experience of those in other villages, that they would take most of the young men away for forced labour in Germany, so we fled into the woods just before they arrived. Since then, we've been making a nuisance of ourselves, though never with the Germans in local villages. We only attack passing convoys, blow up bridges and railways, and send as much information as we can gather to the Allied forces. We limited ourselves in this way in order to prevent retaliation against the villages. So far it seems to have worked.'

'Your resistance work is much admired in London,' Callaghan said with genuine admiration.

André nodded. '*Merci, monsieur.*' He glanced up when the young woman came in, carrying two of the steaming cups of coffee, and gave one each to Callaghan and Greaves, merely nodding and smiling silently when they offered their thanks. She then went back outside and returned almost immediately with the other two cups, placing one in front of André, the other at the left-hand side of the table. When she came back a third time, she was carrying a tray containing four plates and the rolls. In silence, she placed the tray in the middle of the table, handed each man a plate, transferred one of the rolls from the tray to her own plate, then pulled up the remaining chair and sat down. Nodding to Callaghan and Greaves, she said in English: 'Eat, please.'

'*Merci, mademoiselle*,' Callaghan and Greaves said simultaneously.

'This is Maxine,' André told them. 'She left the village with me four years ago. She was then only eighteen years old and already my mistress. She has fought by my side ever since and I don't know what I would do without her. She'll slit a German throat or blow out German brains without thinking twice. If you need a guide, she's at your disposal. Now, please, gentlemen, eat.'

As Maxine was already biting into her roll, the three men helped themselves and ate in silence, meanwhile glancing uneasily, first at one another, then at Maxine, who, though only twenty-two years old, seemed much older.

Eventually, putting his empty plate down, André asked: 'So what is your purpose here?'

'Our original brief,' Callaghan replied, 'was to establish a base, lie low and make contact with the Maquis, then work with you to aid the airborne landings scheduled to take place this week in the Orléans Gap. The main task would have been reconnaissance and sabotage, avoiding direct confrontation wherever possible. However, this morning, just before you returned, we received a coded radio message informing us that the airborne operation has been cancelled. Because of this, because General Patton's advance on Dijon is continuing, and because we're already here and can't go back, we've been ordered to include aggressive patrolling in our future activities in this area.'

'Did your brief include how to deal with us?'

'With your group in particular or the Maquis in general?'

'The Maquis in general.'

'Yes. We were told to try to unite the various local groups and use their pooled intelligence about German locations, activities and troop movements. In return for this, we were to supply you with all the weapons and equipment you need, as well as the benefit of our military experience.'

André nodded and smiled for the first time, though the smile was world-weary and slightly mocking. 'It's nice to know that we'll receive the benefit of your superior military expertise.'

'I'm sorry, André,' Callaghan said. 'I didn't mean to insult the invaluable work being carried out by your group – and, of course, the others. But as you yourself have admitted, your activities have been restricted to relatively minor raids, ambushes and acts of sabotage. What we need now are more ambitious plans and greatly increased manpower and supplies. That's why we're here.'

'But the Maquis already aid the British and receive supplies, weapons and other kinds of aid from them, courtesy of the SOE.'

'Not enough,' Greaves said firmly, since he was the man who had to deal with the Special Operations Executive, a duty that he found frustrating and even counter-productive.

'You mean, not enough in view of the fact that the liberation of Europe has commenced,' André said sarcastically.

'I mean that precisely,' Greaves said. 'The more united we are, the more powerful we are – and the quicker this war comes to an end. It's in your own interests.'

André nodded solemnly, his face serious now. Maxine, sitting to his left, was still nibbling her roll, sipping her hot coffee and listening intently. A petite brunette with delicate features, she did not, to Callaghan's experienced eye, look like the type who could slit throats, German or otherwise.

'So do you have SOE backing for this?' André asked.

'No,' Callaghan replied honestly. 'We have the official backing of 1st Airborne Division and 21st Army Group. We have the discreet, though reluctant, backing of SOE.'

'Why reluctant?'

'Because the SOE sees the Maquis as its own concern. Because it has its own teams to carry out such tasks, it doesn't approve of the SAS arming and organizing Resistance groups.'

'But you insist that you can do it better,' André said.

'Yes. The SAS is widely experienced at insertion, supply and aggressive action behind enemy lines. Therefore, if we linked up with the Maquis, we could accomplish an awful lot together.'

André nodded again, though his smile remained sardonic. When the rumble of Allied aircraft flying to the front became too loud to speak, everyone glanced up automatically. Only when the sound of the aircraft had faded away did they return their attention to the matter in hand.

'So your aim,' André said, 'is to unite the numerous local Maquis groups and place them under a single command, preferably your own.'

'Correct. For the good of all, André.'

The Maquis leader sighed. 'That may not be so easy, Captain. Unfortunately – and I am loath to admit this – the Maquis are split between the supporters of General de Gaulle's Free French and the communists. It sickens me to say so, but the latter regard de Gaulle as no more than the puppet of the British and Americans. They'll use him now – but they've made it perfectly clear that they'll discard him the instant they feel they can do so safely.'

'Yes,' Callaghan said. 'We've heard of the problems caused by that division, but we feel we can live with it and still benefit. How serious do you think it is?'

'Serious enough. Sadly, many Maquisards are more interested in storing weapons for after the war, when they intend to settle scores with de Gaulle's supporters. Frankly, they're more interested in that than they are in killing the Germans.'

'That explains why there are traitors in your midst.'

'Yes, I fear it does. With that fact you will have to learn to live – as indeed we do.'

'I'm willing to try it.'

Now looking more friendly, André, after glancing at Maxine, said: 'I can only assure you, Captain, that apart from the problems mentioned, you will find my men – I can only speak for my own, of course – well organized and highly motivated. If you're willing to try this, you'll have their full co-operation. I personally guarantee it.'

'Thank you, André.'

Both men shook hands across the table, then the Maquis leader pulled a packet of cigarettes from his jacket pocket and passed them round. Everyone lit up and puffed contentedly, including Maxine, who, sounding surprisingly sure of herself, despite her imperfect English, asked: 'So what happens now that you are here?'

Noticing that she was smiling and appeared charming, after all – suddenly realizing, in effect, just how young she really was – the Englishmen both relaxed.

'The first thing,' Callaghan said, 'is to bring in the rest of the equipment required for both groups – by which I mean the SAS and the Maquis. This will include tents for my men, decent food, more weapons and ammunition, and anything that your people may require. I'll brief my men in the morning, once they've had a proper rest, and arrange for the first drop tomorrow night at a DZ chosen by you. Once the supplies have arrived, we'll convert this tent city into a proper forward operating base, although still in tents, with ringed fortifications and good communications. Should all go well, we'll then be in a position to immeasurably aid the Allied advance through France. What do you say?'

André stared gravely at Callaghan and Greaves, glanced at his smiling girlfriend, then reached into another pocket and withdrew a hip-flask. Uncorking it, he poured its contents into each of the empty coffee cups. He then raised his cup in a toast and the others did the same.

'Calvados,' he explained, then at last smiled and said: 'Welcome, gentlemen! To friendship.'

6

Taking advantage of what Callaghan viewed as a day of rest, the men of C Squadron spent the morning cleaning and checking the firing mechanisms of their weapons, the afternoon studying maps of the area with the help of the Maquis, and then were called to an open-air briefing around five o'clock. Already exhausted, they squatted on the spare ground between their LUPs and the Maquisards' tents while the seemingly inexhaustible Captain Callaghan, with Captain Greaves by his side, told them about the recent change in plans.

'So,' Callaghan summarized, after telling them what he had already told André Flaubert, 'with the airborne landings cancelled, we can forget lying low and instead embark on a series of aggressive patrols.'

The men spontaneously began to clap, cheer and whistle, bringing a smile to the faces of both officers, who knew that the very idea of 'passive action' had been frustrating them. When the noise had subsided, which it did only after Sergeant Lorrimer bawled for silence, Callaghan continued.

'Our main tasks are to cut railway lines used as German supply routes or for troop movements, cause general disruption to enemy MSRs, respond to requests from 21st Army Group, 1st Airborne Group, SOE and our own HQ back at Moor Park for information that will help them select targets for Allied bombing raids, and, when not specifically engaged in a task for the aforementioned, simply go out and attack German convoys or FOBs.'

This last remark caused another outburst of jubilation, which was instantly silenced by Lorrimer. When the noise had subsided, the ever-thoughtful Sergeant Bob Tappman asked: 'Do we operate under instructions from 21st Army Group, 1st Airborne Group or the SOE?'

'We operate under instructions from all three, but only when they have a specific task for us. Otherwise, we're on our own and can choose our own targets.'

Another bout of cheering was silenced when Bob Tappman asked: 'Do we make direct attacks on our own initiative?'

'Yes. Aggressive patrolling is now the order of the day. When not set a specific task by SOE, 21st Army Group or our own HQ, we're to attack the enemy where seen and, if possible, destroy their armoured vehicles with our Bofors anti-tank guns.'

'That's my kind of music!' Jacko said, laughing.

'What about communications?' It was Bob Tappman again, thoroughgoing as ever.

'Arrangements have been made for instructions or information to be received from, or sent to, Great Britain in a number of ways. One is the time-honoured use of homing pigeons carrying maps or coded information that will either help our bombers locate their targets or guide us to new targets for our hit-and-run raids.'

'Pigeons!' Harry-boy Turnball breathed melodramatically. 'We're back in the Dark Ages!'

'That's only one system,' Callaghan responded, unperturbed, 'and it's certainly more effective than you can imagine. Pigeons don't get shot out of the sky like aircraft and they don't argue like agents on the ground. In short, they're reliable.'

'The man's faith in human nature is amazing!' Jacko whispered to Rich.

'It's positively inspiring,' Rich whispered back. 'It gives me hope to go on.'

'Naturally,' Callaghan said, 'we'll continue to rely on the field radio, utilizing Morse code. But coded messages will also be put out by the BBC and received by our signallers working in the field with the resistance forces on various types of miniature receiver, such as the MCR1, known and loved by you all as the "biscuit receiver".' Callaghan was referring to the fact that the MCR1 was small enough to be slotted into a Huntley & Palmer's biscuit tin that also contained an additional three batteries and five miniature valves. 'However,' he continued, 'having learnt to our cost that German D/F – direction finding to the uninitiated – has become frighteningly efficient, it's recommended that those of you using the receivers change location and frequency as often as possible, to avoid being tracked down. You should also keep your transmissions as brief as possible. To help in this, a series of 600 four-letter codes has been devised and printed out on large silk scarves. Each of you – not just the signallers – will be supplied with one of these scarves and you're expected to carry it on your person at all times.'

'I always wanted a silk scarf,' Jacko said loudly. 'Now I can walk with a wiggle!'

'You'll get my boot up your arse if you do,' Lorrimer growled at him. 'Now shut up and let the boss get on with it.'

'What about air support?' Bob Tappman asked.

'No problem. As part of 1st Airborne Division, we've been promised strong support from the RAF, including the use of the Lancasters, Halifaxes, Stirlings and Dakotas of 38 Group, as well as others from 46 Group and the Special Duty Squadron based at Tempsford in Bedfordshire. If necessary, these will be supplemented by gliders. Supplies will include not only general kit, food and light weapons, but heavy-duty vehicles such as Bedford QL trucks, the latest, modified four-wheel-drive Willys jeeps, and the Bofors six-pounder anti-tank guns required for the task just mentioned.'

'Excuse me, boss,' Rich asked, 'but we all think the Willys jeeps are fine as they are, so how have they been modified?'

'Nothing that should bother you,' Callaghan replied, 'and a lot that should please you. The latest model is fitted with special armoured plating across the front bumper. That modified bumper has a wire-cutting device fixed to it. Another innovation is bulletproof Perspex screens in front of the driver and front gunner. The old condensers have been removed to enable reserve fuel tanks to be fitted under the driver's seat and over the lockers at the back, giving the jeep a range of over 600 miles. The new jeeps, like the previous models, are fitted with twin Vickers .303-inch K guns front and rear, but these now have heavier tubular-steel mountings. In addition, a fifth K gun has been mounted beside the driver, enabling him to fire while still driving with one hand.'

'I love it!' Jacko exclaimed.

'As the K guns can empty their 100-round magazines in half a second,' Callaghan continued, grinning at Jacko's enthusiasm, 'shooting tracer, armour-piercing and incendiary bullets, and rounds of ball ammunition, this additional gun for the driver has turned the jeep into a formidable mobile fighting unit. I think you will indeed love it.'

'Just let me at it!' the cocky Neil Moffatt called out.

'Also included with the weaponry for each jeep,' Callaghan continued briskly, knowing he had won the men's hearts, 'are a Bren gun for firing outside the jeep, grenades for dropping over the rear to deter pursuers and, of course, either a 9mm Sten sub-machine-gun or a tommy-gun as a personal weapon – you can make your own choice. Finally, for the purposes of communication, each jeep comes with a No. 11 radio, already mounted, and a set of S-phones and Eureka beacons which, being compact and lightweight, can be carried easily when you're out of the vehicle.'

'Do we use the radio for communication with our air support?' Bob Tappman asked.

'No,' Callaghan replied. 'Its transmissions take too long and could be picked up by the German D/F, so we'll only use it for on-the-ground communications. For anything else, particularly air support, we'll be using the S-phones and Eureka beacons. The former can be detected at a distance of up to six miles by an aircraft flying at 10,000 feet, while the latter can be picked up from up to forty miles away by any aircraft equipped with Rebecca radar. Even better, by using a narrow emission beam and ultrashort waves, both systems are virtually invisible to enemy D/F.'

'Can I take it we'll be working with the Maquis, boss?' Bob Tappman asked.

'Yes.'

'That could be tricky.'

'Yes. For one thing, they don't know too much about keeping under cover – they still tend to gather in large, noisy groups. More importantly, they're split between the supporters of de Gaulle and the communists, which means their network is riddled with traitors. We therefore have to be extremely careful when engaged in joint operations with them. If, for instance, they pick a DZ for us, we'll use it because of their knowledge of the local area – which means it will basically be a safe DZ – but we'll do so in the full awareness that it might have been compromised by a traitor passing on information about the drop to the Germans. What I'm saying is that I'm expecting a high level of co-operation between us and the Maquis, and that I believe them to be well organized and highly motivated in general, with invaluable local knowledge, but that the divisions between them, including their communist and Nazi sympathizers, could lead to dangerous complications. In short, respect them but treat them with caution. Finally, I should warn you that although you'll be wearing uniforms, the fact that you're working with the Maquis will get you branded as agents by the Germans.'

'What's the difference?' Jacko asked, being serious for once.

'The difference,' Callaghan told him bluntly, 'is that if the Krauts catch you, they'll ignore the rules of war, probably torture you for information, and almost certainly have you executed as enemy agents rather than soldiers.'

'So we don't let them catch us,' Jacko said.

'Precisely, Lance-Corporal.' Callaghan shifted his uncommonly direct gaze from Jacko to the other men. 'Any specific questions, gentlemen?'

'Yes, boss,' Harry-boy said, putting up his hand to be noticed, as if back in the schoolroom. 'When do we start?'

'Immediately. In fact, the first supplies are being dropped in about half an hour – ten minutes after last light – and I want you out there to collect the containers. I'm taking you there myself to show you how it's done. So get off your backsides and let's go. I want you in full battle kit in the Maquis transport five minutes from now.'

'Hop it!' Lorrimer bawled.

The open-air meeting broke up and the men hurried back to their LUPs to collect their webbing and weapons. Once kitted out, they hurried to the black Citroën vans and nondescript trucks used by the Maquis instead of jeeps because they reduced the chances of being stopped by German patrols. When everyone was in a vehicle, the column moved out of the camp, following a Citroën van which contained Captains Callaghan and Greaves and, right behind it, a similar vehicle carrying André Flaubert, Maxine, and other Maquisards, including a few women, to a drop zone some two miles from the camp.

They reached the DZ ten minutes later. There, in a huge field about 1000 yards long, watched carefully by the SAS troops, the Maquisards piled brushwood up in three piles approximately 100 yards apart to form an L shape, then poured the contents of cans of petrol over them. As they were doing so, some of the SAS men were dispatched to point positions north, south, east and west, first to check that no Germans were waiting in ambush and then to keep their eyes peeled for the enemy in general. Meanwhile, Callaghan, with his signalling torch in his hand, walked off to take up a position thirty yards to the west of the three brushwood beacons. His signaller, Corporal Jim Almonds, had removed his S-phone from its aluminium box and was clipping it to the webbing on his chest, preparing to use it both as a homing beacon for the incoming Dakota and as a radio-telephone link with the plane's radio operator.

'When the incoming aircraft crosses the right angle formed by the brushwood piles and the recognition signal flashed by Captain Callaghan,' Captain Greaves explained to his men, 'the pilot will know he's at the DZ, flying into the wind, and can order his loadmaster to drop the supplies. Naturally, this is a system devised by the Maquis in the absence of proper equipment. When the Dakota drops its supplies, we'll be able to use the same set-up for other DZs, but with three red lights instead of the bonfires and a proper white light for flashing Morse instead of this torch. Got that?'

'Got it, boss,' Rich said.

'Good. Now I want you men to stand at regular intervals along both sides of the DZ – west and east of it – ready to run in and collect the containers being dropped by parachute. Clear the field before the aircraft makes its second pass to drop some more of our men. OK, get going.'

Running with their backs to the wind, which was blowing strongly, but facing the anticipated direction of the incoming plane, the SAS troopers took up their positions at regular intervals in two long lines either side of the DZ. Once in position, they divided their attention between watching for the Dakota, keeping their eyes peeled for Germans beyond the guarded perimeter of the field, and waiting for the Maquisards to set fire to the piles of brushwood. Though the resistance fighters waiting by the beacons included some young, attractive women, the SAS men kept their thoughts to themselves and did not make the usual chauvinistic remarks. Indeed, they were all as quiet as mice and the only sound to be heard until the plane came in was the wind's soft moaning.

Eventually, after what was only five minutes though it seemed much longer, Callaghan heard the distant drone of an approaching plane and instantly alerted Corporal Almonds, who plugged in the short-directional aerial of his S-phone. This would send out a beam that would vibrate the needle of the direction indicator on the controls of the incoming Dakota, enabling the pilot to fly directly towards the source of the signal. At the same time, the Maquisards lit blazing torches and threw them on to the three petrol-soaked piles of brushwood, which burst into flames and were soon burning fiercely.

This was the most dangerous part of the operation because the beacons could be seen a long way off and reveal the men's presence to passing German patrols. As a result, they grew increasingly nervous and wary as they waited for the aircraft.

Eventually it appeared in the southern sky, homing in on Almonds's S-phone and heading directly for the beacons. As it did so, Callaghan flashed a Morse confirmation that the DZ was clear. A back-up confirmation conveyed by the signaller's S-phone brought the aircraft right in over the DZ and the first of the canisters floated down beneath billowing white parachutes.

When the canisters had all landed, with their collapsed parachutes being whipped dramatically by the wind and the Dakota circling around to come back for the second drop, the SAS men on both sides of the DZ rushed in to collect them. The sheet-metal cylinders were all some six feet long, though there were two different kinds: C-type and H-type. The former contained weapons and clothing, packed carefully to fill the whole of their length, while the latter each held five smaller cylinders, locked together with restraining rods and carrying ammunition, rations and other supplies.

After sliding a thick wooden pole through each pair of carrying handles on the cylinders, some of the SAS men, in teams of four, carried the C-type containers away from the DZ and loaded them into the back of the Maquis trucks. To remove the H-type canisters from the field, they released the restraining rods, separated the five smaller cylinders, and carried them by straps slipped through their carrying rings.

A few minutes later the Dakota returned for its second drop, but this time it disgorged hampers, panniers, and even wicker baskets containing radio spares. Finally, when the aircraft made its third run, twelve more SAS paratroopers drifted down. As soon as they hit the ground, they were met by their comrades and escorted to the waiting trucks, which drove them away even as the Dakota was disappearing in the dark sky on its way back to England.

The men still in the field climbed back into the Maquis vehicles to be driven the two miles back to the camp. Once there, they emptied the containers, then buried them in ditches dug for the purpose and covered the upturned earth with foliage.

Fully equipped, they were now all set to attack.

7

The modified Willys jeeps were dropped by a Halifax the following night and quickly assembled by the SAS troopers. The original jeeps were passed on to the Maquis and at first light the next morning the SAS, guided by André, Maxine and a handful of other Maquisards, were on the road, looking for targets.

As before, they broke up into three columns and headed off in different directions, having agreed to meet up every two hours at a forest RV near the town of Châtillon. Group One was led by the jeep containing André, Maxine and two other male members of the Maquis. Directly behind the lead jeep was the one containing Sergeant Lorrimer, Jacko and Rich, with five more jeeps behind them, the last two filled with Maquisards.

Having left the camp just as the sun was rising over the green hills, they were soon racing along a road that wound pleasantly around hilly fields, between dense stands of birch trees and tall hedgerows. The roads and fields seemed empty, but the men knew that this appearance could be deceptive as skirmishes were taking place to the north, south and east, beyond the horizon, and in any case the movement of German troops was unpredictable. They were reminded of the larger war by the frequent passage of Allied bombers and, depending on the direction in which the constantly winding road took them, by the smoke darkening the sky to the east where General Patton's 3rd Army was advancing despite strong resistance.

As he passed a farmer in a horse-drawn cart – the first soul they had seen since setting out forty minutes earlier – André slowed down, ran alongside him and asked if the next village was clear of Germans. The farmer nodded. Hoping to pick up information about enemy movements from the villagers, André drove on with the rest of the column strung out behind him.

A sharp bend in the road led abruptly into the single street of a picturesque village, where a bunch of Afrika Korps troops were spilling out of a truck, probably intending to stretch their legs. Slamming his foot on the brake, André went into a brief, noisy skid and screeched to a halt, the jeeps behind doing the same.

Instantly, the Germans scattered to both sides of the road and behind their truck, unslinging their rifles on the move. The first shots were fired before the SAS and the Maquisards could get out of their vehicles – a fusillade that peppered André's jeep and blew out the front tyres. Even as bullets were ricocheting off the vehicle, the two men in the back were jumping out. André and Maxine scrambled over the rear seats to do the same.

Jacko's twin Vickers roared into action as he gave the men in the first jeep covering fire with a savage, sustained burst, swinging the weapon from left to right, cutting down the enemy soldiers still racing across the road. They screamed, dropped their weapons, flung their hands up, spun away and collapsed in clouds of dust. The survivors frantically pressed themselves flat against the front doors of the stone houses lining the street and returned Jacko's fire.

Behind Jacko, Rich let rip with his own machine-gun, aiming at the Germans on the left side of the road, spraying the walls around them with bullets, showering them with dust and flying fragments of stone. Meanwhile Lorrimer was kneeling behind the jeep, swinging in and out constantly to pick off individual Germans with short, deadly bursts from his 9mm Sten gun.

As André and Maxine dropped to the ground behind their vehicle, between the other two Maquisards, both of whom were leaning out to fire their rifles at the Germans shooting at them from behind their truck, the few civilians still in the street either threw themselves to the ground or bolted for cover into the nearest house or shop.

The SAS men not manning the mounted machine-guns were either firing their weapons from behind the jeeps or boldly darting across the road, dodging the whipping lines of dust created by German bullets, to take up positions in vacant doorways, from where they had an oblique view of the Germans hiding behind the truck. Having taken careful aim with their Sten guns and tommy-guns, they unleashed a hail of fire that cut down many of the Germans and forced the rest to flee from behind the truck and try to reach either side of the road, and the shelter of the doorways.

Few made it. Caught in a fusillade that turned the road into a storm of spitting dust and flying stones, most of them were cut down within seconds, screaming, shuddering, spinning and falling to the ground. The few who managed to reach cover failed to find the protection they had sought. Jacko and Rich had taken opposite sides of the road and were pouring a murderous hail of fire from their machine-guns into the doorways, so that the Germans trying to fire from there were blinded and choked by the dust and debris thrown up by the stream of bullets. As they leant forward gingerly to see and breathe properly, they were savagely cut down.

At that moment, Lorrimer unclipped the pin of a 36 hand-grenade and hurled it at the rear of the troop truck. The grenade looped upward in a languid arc, then fell into the back of the vehicle. Less than a second later, it exploded, blowing the canvas covering to shreds, setting the flying tatters on fire and buckling the exposed metal supports. Simultaneously, the petrol tank exploded with a deafening roar, creating an inferno of yellow flames and boiling black smoke, from which emerged two screaming Germans, both on fire and quivering epileptically as they slumped to the ground.

'Go after them!' Lorrimer yelled, jabbing his finger to indicate both sides of the street, where the few remaining German soldiers were scurrying into the houses.

As the SAS troops inched along both sides of the street, darting from door to door, the eight Maquisards from the last two jeeps split into two groups and hurried behind the houses, intent on stopping the Germans making their escape by the back doors.

'The top floors!' Lorrimer bawled as he dropped back on his haunches and aimed his Sten gun up at the top window of one of the houses. His short, controlled burst blew out the window, where a shadowy figure had appeared, and the figure dropped back out of sight. Lorrimer then jumped up and ran towards the houses on his right, following André and Maxine and screaming over his shoulder to Jacko and Rich: 'Keep manning those guns!' Frustrated, Jacko and Rich had to remain in the jeep while Lorrimer and other troopers rushed into the houses, kicking in doors where necessary, and began to flush out the remaining Germans as the occupants huddled in panic behind the furniture.

As the SAS men were entering the houses, following the example set by André and Maxine, most of the remaining German soldiers were fleeing through the back doors – where they were cut down by the Maquisards waiting for them. Lorrimer heard the harsh chatter of their lethal gunfire as he raced through the small living-room of the house he had entered, then saw the frantically jabbing finger of the white-faced housewife, indicating that a German soldier was upstairs.

Aware that the villagers could ill afford the damage being inflicted on their houses, but knowing too that it was unavoidable, Lorrimer went carefully to the stairs, looked up, saw nothing, then started to ascend as quietly as possible. He was halfway up when, to his relief, he heard the loud chatter of a Schmeisser being fired from inside the front bedroom. The noise drowned his footfall on the creaking stairs as he covered the last treads and turned into the short, gloomy hallway.

An Afrika Korps trooper was at the window of the bedroom to Lorrimer's left, firing down on the men in the street. Temporarily deafened by the roar of his machine-gun, he did not hear the SAS man until it was too late. At that point he jerked his head around, saw Lorrimer aiming at him, and tried to turn his whole body so as to fire his weapon. Lorrimer's burst took him in the chest, punching him back against the window frame, which rattled violently, and turning his tunic into a bloody rag. Bouncing off the wall, he flopped face down on the floor as his Schmeisser clattered noisily across the bare boards.

Lorrimer checked that he was dead, then went downstairs and said in his halting French to the frightened woman: 'I'm sorry. Don't go up there. Wait until we come back for the body. We'll be as quick as possible.'

The woman was speechless with fright and merely nodded at Lorrimer as he went back into the street. Short bursts of gunfire could still be heard from behind the houses on both sides, but most of the SAS and resistance fighters were now coming out of the houses, having killed off any snipers found inside.

Lorrimer was learning from Rich that there were no SAS or Maquis casualties when two Afrika Korps troopers emerged from a house with their hands up, being covered by André and the delicate-featured Maxine. The Maquis leader was carrying the Germans' Schmeissers in his free hand. When they were back on the road, near the smouldering ruins of the troop truck blown up by Lorrimer's grenade, Maxine kept them covered with her American M1 carbine as André questioned them about the strength and movements of other German units in the area. When both men refused to answer, Maxine placed the barrel of her weapon against the back of the head of one of them.

'Talk or I shoot,' she said in German.

Both men shook their heads.

Maxine pressed the trigger and the German's head exploded into a torrent of blood and flying bone as his body convulsed and collapsed.

'What the hell . . .!' Outraged and red-faced, Sergeant Lorrimer marched up to André and Maxine and glared at each of them in turn. 'That man was our prisoner!' he bawled.

'He refused to talk,' Maxine said quietly. 'You can rest assured that this one will.' Then, unconcerned by Lorrimer's rage, she placed the barrel of her carbine against the second soldier's head.

'Talk or I shoot,' she said.

The German started babbling to André, who listened attentively while Lorrimer, disgusted, hurried off to give his men further instructions.

'Jesus Christ, did you see that?' Jacko asked Rich, both of them still standing at their mounted machine-guns.

'Christ, yes! She didn't hesitate for a second – just blew his brains out.'

'Bloody barbaric,' Jacko said, spitting over the side of the jeep.

'She's such a sweet-looking young thing,' Rich said, studying Maxine with disbelieving eyes. 'You'd think butter wouldn't melt in her mouth . . . And then she does that.'

'Fucking hard life in the Maquis. If they're caught, the Germans routinely torture them before executing them. That knowledge toughens them up.'

'I'll say it does!'

'All right, stop your jabbering,' Lorrimer told them when he reached the jeep. 'We're not finished yet. Listen to me, everyone!' he bawled down the column. 'I want one man to remain in the jeep, manning a machine-gun. The others are to form two-man teams and go back into the houses to drag out any dead Germans you find there.' He waited for the inevitable groans to die away, then continued: 'When you bring the dead out, line them up along the street near the blacksmith's . . . *Corporal Almonds!*'

'Yes, Sarge!' the signaller called back from the radio jeep.

'We can't have these Krauts stinking up the village and maybe causing disease, so get on the radio and tell base camp to send out a burial detail.'

'Will do, Sarge!'

'All right, men, get to it.'

Most of the SAS men tossed coins to determine who would stay in the jeep and who would get the less pleasant job of gathering up the dead. As the losers were dispersing, muttering under their breath, the Maquisards who had gone round the back of the same houses, to cut down the Germans trying to escape that way, appeared around the corners at both ends of the short street, walking backwards with their weapons slung over their shoulders, dragging the German dead by their feet. Lorrimer told them to use the area in front of the blacksmith's. Eventually, the SAS men had dragged out the others and the many blood-soaked dead were lying on their backs in the street, being studied by the curious, often delighted, villagers.

'So,' Lorrimer said to André, still furious with them both. 'Did you get anything valuable out of the prisoner you didn't execute?'

'A little, but not much,' said André. 'I think he genuinely didn't know much about anything other than the plans for his own squadron.'

'So the other one died in vain.'

'We all do, Sergeant.'

'And what have you done with the survivor?'

André pointed to inside the blacksmith's shop, where the prisoner was resting on the ground, his hands and legs tied, one of the Maquisards keeping him covered with an M1 carbine. 'My man will protect him from the wrath of the villagers, then hand him over to the SAS burial party when they arrive.'

'Good,' Lorrimer replied, only slightly mollified. 'Let's move on.'

The column moved out of the village, leaving behind the German dead and the grateful, cheering residents. Almost immediately the jeeps were back in the narrow lane that wound in a leisurely manner between smooth, green hills and tall hedgerows. The sun was now high in the sky and the birds were singing lustily. Only the smoke staining the blue sky in the distance reminded them that the war was still being fought at that very moment.

'A nice little drive,' Jacko said, sitting beside his Vickers, which was now in the locked position, its barrel pointing skyward. 'A pleasant day in the country.'

'Apart from nearly getting our balls shot off, it's been *very* pleasant,' said Rich, who was now likewise sitting relaxed, though his dark eyes remained watchful.

'At least it's better than North Africa,' Jacko said. 'Lots more to see. Not least some pretty French fillies. Does the heart good, that does.'

They're supposed to be pretty liberal, aren't they?' Rich asked doubtfully.

'So they say. At least, they think the English are a bunch of puritans by comparison, so they must be pretty quick off the mark when it comes to pulling their knickers down. I wouldn't mind a taste of it.'

'Maybe when we get leave.'

'In Paris,' Jacko said.

'I always wanted to see Paris,' Rich revealed, 'and I can't wait to get there.'

'I wouldn't argue with that. Cheap cognac, naughty night-clubs and fast fillies. That'll do me, mate.'

The roar of a 75mm gun cut short their conversation as the jeep turned a corner. Both men ducked instinctively when the shell whistled over their heads and exploded between them and the jeep behind, showering them with soil, stones and grass as the blast slammed their jeep forward into the ditch by the side of the road.

As the other jeeps screeched to a halt at both sides of the road, spilling out their men, Lorrimer, Jacko and Rich crawled from their wrecked vehicle and wriggled down into the ditch, between darting, spitting lines of dust kicked up by a torrent of machine-gun bullets. Looking up, they saw a good number of German troops advancing boldly from a sandbagged gun emplacement at the side of the road, most firing Schmeissers from the hip.

More bullets ricocheted around them, shredding the foliage and making the dirt spit in jagged lines as Jacko and Rich unslung their tommy-guns. Hearing a scream, Lorrimer glanced behind him and saw that one of the Maquisards had been hit and was rolling on to his back, grabbing frantically at his smashed and bloody kneecap. The SAS troops beyond him were either resting on one knee or were down on their bellies, firing at the advancing Germans.

'*Bring up some Bren guns*!' Lorrimer bawled as a medic crawled towards the wounded man.

The sergeant turned back to the front as a big, blond German ran straight towards him, firing from the hip. As Jacko and Rich were still disentangling the personal weapons slung across their shoulders, Lorrimer raised his Sten gun and fired a burst into the advancing soldier. The giant screamed, convulsed, dropped his weapon and clutched his stomach, then pitched forward into the dirt.

Nevertheless, more German troops were advancing along the edge of the field on the other side of the hedgerow, which their relentless fire was tearing to shreds. The bullets tore up soil and dust around Lorrimer and his men, and leaves and smashed branches showered down on them. The noise was atrocious.

Spitting dirt and rubbing it from their eyes, Neil and Harry-boy crawled past the wounded, screaming Maquisard as Jacko and Rich opened fire with their tommy-guns.

Squinting through a gap in the hedgerow, Lorrimer saw that the road bent back almost at a right angle and that the last two of his jeeps were parked there, with the men clambering out and clearly about to crawl around to the front. Wanting to use those same men to attack the German flank instead, he shouted to Neil and Harry-boy: 'Keep those bastards back!' Then he crawled away.

The roar of the two Bren guns joined the noisy chatter of Jacko and Rich's weapons as Lorrimer crawled past the wounded Frenchman, who was quieter now that he was being attended to by the medic.

Another 75mm shell whistled overhead and exploded with a mighty roar between two of the jeeps. No one was hurt, though Lorrimer found himself crawling through swirling dust and soil with a loud, ringing noise in his head.

As the murk cleared, André came into view, jumping up from behind a jeep and swinging his free hand to release a 'potato-masher' – a captured German hand-grenade which had a wooden handle with a screw-on exploding canister at one end. Even as the long, thin device was curving through the air, André was dropping back behind the jeep, beside the petite but murderous Maxine, and firing another burst from his M1 carbine, as his girlfriend was doing.

The potato-masher exploded in the midst of the Germans advancing along the side of the ditch, slamming them in opposite directions, some into the hedgerow, others on to the road, and covering the area in a choking black smoke.

Lorrimer crawled on, passing André and Maxine, until he came to the bend in the road. There, he jumped up and ran at the crouch around the curve to meet the SAS men coming the other way, also crouching and with weapons ready.

'Get back,' he shouted. 'I don't want you at the front. There are more Krauts advancing along the other side of the hedgerow, just down from the gun position. I think we can attack their flank from further along this lane, where it curves sharply back on itself. So turn around and go back the way you came, past your jeeps, until we find a direct line of fire to that gun position. *Now move it!*'

The men, led by Sergeant Bob Tappman and Corporal Benny Bennett, did as they were told and hurried back with Lorrimer around the bend to their jeeps as a German mortar shell exploded nearby, showering them with soil and slapping them with its shock waves. As they passed the jeeps, Lorrimer made the men stop and told Benny to pick up the 2.36-inch bazooka and some 60mm shells. This done, Benny and the others kept going until they came to where the road curved dramatically and gave a direct view across the field to the back of the gun emplacement. It also gave a clear line of fire into the flank of the Germans who were inching their way along the edge of the field and firing through the hedgerow at the SAS and the Maquisards.

'Perfect,' Lorrimer whispered, then turned with a triumphant grin to Sergeant Tappman. 'Bob, set that Bren gun up on its bipod and fire the instant the first shell from the bazooka explodes. Corporal Bennett will fire the bazooka at my command. The rest of you will join the Bren gun in putting a stop to those bastards inching along the field. Let's give them what for, lads.'

While Bob Tappman was setting up his Bren gun, Benny Bennett stretched out on his belly on the ground, rested the relatively light bazooka anti-tank weapon on his right shoulder, loaded it with a 60mm shell, then took hold of the grips and aimed at the centre of the enemy position. Lorrimer waited until both men were ready, then tapped Benny on the shoulder and said: 'Fire!'

The bazooka appeared to explode on Benny's shoulder, spitting a fierce flame, jerking backwards to rock the corporal's whole body, and propelling the shell out of the barrel on a tracery of smoke that showed exactly where the shell was going. It shot in a virtually straight line into the rear of the sandbagged gun emplacement, then exploded with a deafening roar and a force that made the ground shake.

Even as the position was blown apart, with human limbs, twisted metal and sand from the shredded sandbags spinning out and upwards amid clouds of boiling smoke, Bob Tappman was opening fire with his Bren gun, sweeping it left and right to pour his bullets in a long arc into the flank of the Germans advancing along the edge of the field. As he did so, the other SAS men added a murderous hail of fire from their 9mm Sten sub-machine-guns and tommy-guns.

The hedgerow framing the Germans was torn to shreds, leaves raining down and broken branches flying everywhere as they jerked, twisted, shook spasmodically and finally collapsed. Those at the beginning and end of the column managed to run in opposite directions out of the line of fire, but Bob Tappman and his troopers adjusted their aim and had cut them down too within seconds.

When the smoke from the devastated emplacement had cleared, there were only dead Germans in the field to the side of it. The position itself was a mess of burning canvas, smouldering sandbags and charred, lifeless bodies. This side of the field had been brutally, efficiently cleared.

'Now we can cross the field and catch the other Germans on the road between us and the rest of our column,' Lorrimer said. 'Come on, men, let's go.'

While Bob Tappman folded up the bipod of his Bren gun in order to tuck the weapon into his side like an assault rifle, Benny Bennett broke the bazooka in half to make it easier to carry. They and the rest of the men then spread out in a long line, so as to reduce the risk of being hit by enemy fire, and advanced toward the dead Germans sprawled by the hedgerow near the destroyed gun emplacement.

As they advanced across the empty field, they could hear the continuing gunfire from the road on the other side of the hedgerow, where the Germans were still moving slowly along the rim of the ditch. Approaching the hedgerow carefully, the SAS men spread out even more to give themselves individually selected targets. Through gaps in the hedgerow they could see the German soldiers making their painfully slow progress and, further along, the SAS and Maquisards firing at them from behind the parked jeeps.

At a hand signal from Lorrimer, the men fired through the hedgerow, their combined fire-power tearing much of it to shreds and cutting down the Germans on the other side. Taken completely by surprise and shocked by the massacre, the remaining Germans panicked and either jumped down into the ditch or leapt over it on to the road. Either way, they made themselves prime targets.

A minute or so later, the last of the Germans had fallen and silence descended over the road. Lorrimer then led his group around the opening in the hedge, near the wrecked enemy gun position, and back up the road to join the others. Even as he was approaching them, he saw André, Maxine and the other Maquisards giving the *coup de grâce* to the

German wounded. Knowing that he could do nothing to stop them, Lorrimer just looked the other way.

'Let's head for the RV,' he said to Jacko and Rich. 'We've got to get there before dark.'

'We should be sleeping during the day,' Jacko said, 'and fighting at night. Driving about here in broad daylight is crazy. What do you think, Sarge?'

'I think you're right, Jacko.'

When the single Allied casualty, the wounded Maquisard, had been placed in the jeep and the other men were all seated, the column moved off.

8

Arriving at the RV just before sunset, Sergeant Lorrimer's group met up with the other two, headed by Captains Callaghan and Greaves. As they would do for the rest of their sojourn in France, even before making up their bashas the men carried out their customary inspection of the jeeps, checking the oil, water, petrol, carburettors and tyres before the sun set. While they were doing so, Corporal Jim Almonds was using two improvised systems to simultaneously recharge exhausted radio batteries. For some he was using a small windmill mounted on a collapsible ten-foot pole. For others he was using a steam recharger consisting of a boiler hung over a brazier and attached to a portable two-cylinder engine coupled to a generator. The pressure resulting from the steam in the boiler was then used to recharge the six-volt batteries. The signaller was also checking the five miniature tubes, three thirty-hour batteries and MCR1 receivers housed in biscuit tins and generally carried by the men when on foot for clandestine operations.

'Albert bloody Einstein,' Harry-boy Turnball said mockingly as he passed by to have a piss in the bushes.

'Who's he?' said Almonds.

'A Kraut scientist,' Harry-boy informed him, so in love with the idea of being superior that he temporarily forgot his bursting bladder.

'The enemy,' the signaller replied.

'A genius,' Harry-boy corrected him.

'Then how come he's a fucking Kraut,' Almonds asked. 'They're all blockheads, they are.'

'Conquered most of Europe, mate.'

'Soft twats, the Europeans, that's why. Frogs and Eyeties and what have you. Not worth pissing on.'

'Which reminds me,' Harry-boy said. 'I'm going to piss in a hole in the ground, but I should be pissing on you instead.'

'What have *I* done?' Almonds asked.

'It's not you; it's your mother.'

'What's me mum got to do with this?'

'She gave birth to you, you daft arsehole.' Harry-boy said, then strode off to empty his bladder.

Ignoring the banter, Sergeant Lorrimer reported to Captain Callaghan, who was sitting with Captain Greaves in the shade of a tree, comparing notes and checking maps. When Lorrimer had reported his group's activities of the day, Callaghan said: 'Not much different to ours. We ran into Jerry wherever we turned and went up against mortars and machine-guns. I was told they only travelled by night, but clearly that's rubbish.'

'Right, boss,' Lorrimer replied. 'Even Jacko – Lance-Corporal Dempster – said we should start going out on patrol only at night, and I think he's right.'

'What do you think, Dirk?' Callaghan asked Greaves.

'I agree. The very idea that Jerry would only travel by night is patently ridiculous. Allied aircraft are pounding their main positions night and day, so they're moving whenever they can and doing it in every damn direction. About the only constant in this fluctuating picture is the knowledge that they're all hoping to get to Germany in the end. Apart from that, they're certainly on the move twenty-four hours a day, which means that we can use the benefit of darkness.'

'Fine,' Callaghan said. 'We're all agreed on that. We'll take tonight and tomorrow off, then move out again tomorrow night. Otherwise we'll use the same tactics, mainly hit-and-run.'

'I'm not sure about having three different groups, though,' Greaves said. 'I had four separate encounters with Jerry today and lost three jeeps in the process. You lost two jeeps, boss. What about you, Sergeant Lorrimer?'

'One.'

'Lucky man!'

'But you're right, Dirk,' Callaghan said. 'That's six jeeps down in the first day – and that's too many for my liking. So I agree that we should divide into two instead of three groups. Do you agree, Sergeant?'

Though Lorrimer was far from being the only sergeant in the squadron, he was treated as virtually a second in command because he was one of the Originals. 'Yes,' he said, 'I do.'

'That means I command one group,' Callaghan pointed out, 'and Captain Greaves the other.'

'Agreed,' Lorrimer told him.

Relieved, both officers glanced out of their natural shelter to where the rest of the men, in gathering darkness, having checked their vehicles, weapons and other kit, including radios, were starting to put up their personal choice of basha. The simpler option was a hollow scraped out of the earth and covered with a roof of thatch and wire. The other type of basha was a simple lean-to, to construct which two

Y-shaped sticks were hammered into the earth and a crossbar, usually the branch of a tree, was placed horizontally between them and hooked into the upright Y shapes. A waterproof poncho was then draped over the branch, with the long end facing the wind and the short end tied to the ground with the cords attached to its edges. Inside both kinds of basha, a sleeping bag was unrolled on the ground. Foliage was then spread over the top of the basha so that it blended in with the surroundings, especially when viewed from the air.

As soon as they had finished their bashas, the men began to open their cold rations. Hot food was permitted only during the day, when the flames from the hexamine stoves could not be seen by the enemy.

'What about the Maquis?' Lorrimer asked.

Without thinking, Callaghan and Greaves glanced at each other, then both looked at the sergeant.

'Why do you ask?' said Callaghan.

'Frankly, boss, I think our views are so different that we won't be able to work comfortably together. The Maquis have had, shall we say, a more . . . *intimate* contact with Jerry than we have. I mean, they've had relations and friends captured, tortured and killed, so they tend to ignore the rules of war. This morning, during our first engagement, one of them, a woman, cold-bloodedly shot a prisoner in the back of the head just to scare another into talking. The second German talked all right, but I don't think it's the kind of thing we should be encouraging, let alone allow the men to see.'

'Did you try talking to them about it?' Callaghan asked.

'I did, but it made no impression on them. Obviously they thought I was soft. Anyway I have my doubts that we can exercise any kind of control over the Maquis – and that could make them dangerous to us. So I say let's consider not sharing any further missions with them.'

'I'm inclined to agree with that,' Greaves said. 'Not only for those reasons, but for others.'

'Such as?' Callaghan asked him.

'Already there have been fights between the Maquis in our group because some of the weapons distributed during the resups have disappeared and the de Gaulle supporters believe that the communists have stashed them away for use after the war – against the Gaullists, that is. The communists have denied this, but what can't be denied is that the weapons are missing and both sides now resent each other – which doesn't help when we're trying to plan a raid. The two branches of the Maquis are at each other's throats and that could lead to trouble for us. So, yes, I agree with Sergeant Lorrimer.'

The rumble of aircraft overhead made them all look up. The sky was now nearly dark, with few stars and gathering clouds, but they could see the dimmed lights of what appeared to be a huge armada of heavy bombers, all heading for the front further south. The dark southern horizon was frequently illuminated with silvery flashes, indicating that bombing raids were already under way. Over there it would certainly be hell on earth, but from where they were it looked pretty and dreamlike.

Callaghan sighed. 'Well, I must say I *did* find my particular bunch of Maquisards pretty undisciplined, with a tendency to gather in large groups and make a lot of noise at the wrong moment. Also, when engaging Jerry, they tended to act like a bunch of cowboys, following their own bent instead of sticking to what had been planned between us. I suspect they may have been doing this more than they normally would because their leader, André, wasn't present, being in your group, Sergeant, but it was certainly enough to make me think twice about depending on them too heavily in the future.'

'So what do you propose?' Callaghan asked.

'A loose affiliation. In future, if we must go on raids together, let the Maquis act independently of us, doing their own thing. They will, in effect, become the third group we'd decided not to have because our jeeps are down in numbers already. In other words, Group One headed by me, Group Two by Captain Callaghan, and Group Three, the Maquis under André. In this way we can utilize their local knowledge and considerable talents for clandestine operations without actually trying to operate alongside them.'

'Sounds sensible,' Greaves said.

'I agree,' Lorrimer added.

Glancing at the lights flashing spasmodically on the otherwise dark horizon, Captain Greaves, while thinking the sight was strangely beautiful, knew just how hellish it must be for those on the ground. His own early involvement with the SAS, in its original form as L Detachment, had sprung indirectly from his being wounded in the great battle for Mersa Brega and Tobruk in the Cyrenaica Desert in March 1941. Then acting as an observation officer for the Middle East Headquarters (MEHQ) in Cairo, he had been in the sprawling Allied camp outside Mersa Brega when it was attacked by the combined might of Rommel's Afrika Korps Panzer divisions, with their deadly Mark III and Mark IV tanks, a horde of Ju-87 Stuka dive-bombers, six-wheeled armoured cars and motorized infantry.

When the appalling din of the British ack-ack guns, Bren guns and 0.5-inch Browning machine-guns was added to that of the German big guns and Panzer 55mm and 75mm fire, the noise became an almost palpable pressure around the head and the air filled up with choking, blinding dust, weirdly illuminated by darting flames and exploding flares.

Even now, Greaves could clearly recall the sensation of the ground shaking beneath him from the explosions, the screaming of wounded and dying men, the roaring, banging and rattling of tanks and other armoured vehicles and, to top it all, the demented scream of the Stukas. It had, indeed, been hell on earth – so much so that Greaves had almost been relieved to have his leg shattered by a round of bullets just outside the harbour town of Tobruk, from where he was casualty-evacuated to the hospital in Alexandria, where he first met the former Scots Guard officer and No. 8 Commando lieutenant, David Stirling, the creator and former head of the SAS.

Once L Detachment had gone into action in North Africa, Greaves saw lots more action, much of it extremely dangerous, but none of it could compare for sheer horror to that mighty battle in Cyrenaica. The combination of smoke, dust and infernal noise had been almost unbearable. So, while the distant lights of the present front were bewitching from where he stood, he didn't envy the men suffering under that bombardment.

'So we become night raiders,' Lorrimer said. 'What are your plans, boss? Anything definite?'

'Not really,' Callaghan replied, 'other than to avoid any more accidental encounters with Jerry and only attack him when we can take him by surprise.'

'Which means?' Greaves asked.

'For a start, it means a great deal of avoidance. According to what a French farmer told me this afternoon, there are Panzer troops strung over this whole area, albeit without their armoured vehicles in most cases. I therefore suggest that we leave tomorrow night, at 2200 hours, drive to Semur, find a suitable location for the next RV, then break up to cover as wide an area as possible, returning to the RV before dawn. Once there, we'll decide on the following night's general target area – and so on each day.'

'Each night, to be precise,' Lorrimer said.

'Sounds rather enjoyable, actually,' Greaves put in. 'I have to admit to finding this kind of war pleasurable compared with what we've been through before. A bit like cowboys and Indians.'

'That's a glib way of putting it,' Callaghan told him, 'but I'll admit it's a bit like that. Not your average kind of war.'

There were, as Callaghan well knew, many different kinds of war and this was the kind that he liked most – it was certainly preferable to being one of those foot soldiers beyond the horizon. The uncomfortable truth, he realized, was that while there were certain horrors of war which he could well do without and, in some instances, indeed dreaded, generally speaking he enjoyed being at war and couldn't really imagine living without it. Though happily married, with one son, Callaghan was forced to accept that no matter how much he loved his family, he could never stay at home for long. This was common to many soldiers, he knew, particularly SAS men, but it was something that few of them would admit.

Take Greaves, he thought. Though soon to be a father and clearly in love with his young wife, Mary, it was highly unlikely that he would even have considered giving up the

SAS for her. Like Callaghan – and like most of the other men in the regiment – Greaves was a decent man who simply could not lead a normal life, being constantly hungry for adventure. Indeed, as Callaghan now recalled with a wry smile, being in love with his wife had not stopped Greaves, back in 1941, when still engaged to his sweetheart, from having a brief fling with Frances Beamish, the attractive Royal Army Medical Corps nurse who had ministered to his needs when his broken leg was healing in the Scottish Military Hospital in Alexandria. That brief affair, Callaghan knew, had sprung out of Greaves's insatiable desire for romance and adventure. In fact, for him, love was rather like war: a form of distraction.

Sergeant Lorrimer was no different. Though reportedly happily married with three children, he had confessed to Callaghan that he was always restless at home and couldn't wait to get back to the regiment, particularly if there was a war to be fought. Nor was it an accident that when first approached to join L Detachment, he had been found in Tiger Lil's brothel in Cairo, where he had actually rented a room for the whole of his leave. When asked why he had done so, he had answered with a single word: 'boredom'.

Lorrimer was a man who liked a man's world and had been toughened by it. Though decent, he had his steely side and made it work for him. War may have been hell to some, but Lorrimer loved it. That's what few can admit, Callaghan thought. The love of war, which many insist is uncivilized, is, rightly or wrongly, an ineradicable part of man's nature. Some truths a lot of people would rather reject. Some are too hard to bear.

'So what are our targets for the night raids?' Lorrimer asked.

'Railway lines, trains, airfields, grounded aircraft, radar stations, communications cables, bridges of strategic value, troop convoys, German FOBs, individual vehicles or foot patrols – anything we can attack before Jerry knows what's happening to him. No more direct encounters like those we had today. No flamboyant gestures.'

'Tell that to the Maquis,' Greaves said sardonically. 'They'll be all ears, I'm sure.'

'I'll go and see André right away,' Callaghan said.

'You won't have to,' Lorrimer told him. 'Here he comes with his sweet, murdering girlfriend.'

The Frenchman was emerging from the darkness of the trees, with Maxine by his side, both of them criss-crossed with webbing and spare ammunition, both with M1 carbines in their hands and Lugers holstered at the hip. When they reached the SAS men, they nodded sombrely.

'A very good first day,' André said with more enthusiasm than they had seen in him before. 'So what plans for tomorrow?'

'You thought that was a good day?' Callaghan asked with an ambiguous smile.

'Of course!' the Maquis leader exclaimed, looking almost happy. 'We killed many Germans!'

'And lost six jeeps,' Callaghan reminded him.

'Six jeeps for twenty Germans,' Maxine said, her brown eyes direct and challenging. 'That's a good trade, Captain.'

'It might have been if we'd planned it that way,' Callaghan countered. 'But we didn't, which means it was no gain. It was simply an accident.'

Maxine frowned and glanced at André, who merely shrugged and then returned his gaze to Callaghan. 'There are many beneficial accidents in war, Captain. They should not be disowned.'

'Accidents of any kind should be avoided at all costs, André. Certainly, an accident that just happens to turn out right for us should not be treated as something worth celebrating.'

'I'm confused, Captain. We killed a great many German soldiers, yet you . . .'

'We were lucky, that's all. We didn't plan to kill them. We didn't even plan to attack them. All three groups fought the Germans in self-defence and desperation. We didn't take them by surprise, as a result of planning. We just ran straight into them. That we only lost six jeeps, instead of a lot of men, was extremely fortunate. As for the jeeps, six were anyway too many to lose in the first day. We made a mess of it, André.'

The Frenchman stared at Callaghan as if he couldn't believe his ears, then glanced at Maxine. The young woman's gaze, though remaining steady, was more intense than before. It was a look of pure anger.

'Shit!' she exploded. 'That's what you're trying to give us! You turn our triumph into a turd because you want to control us. Well, Captain, it won't work. We know too much for that. You come here as our liberators, filled with the confidence of the free, but you don't know a damn thing. *We* know! We have borne witness for years. We know how the Germans think, what they will do, and we react accordingly. You do not like to see Germans executed? Unplanned firefights disturb you? Then get out of our way, Captain Callaghan, and let us win the war our way.'

'I don't think I can do that,' Callaghan replied calmly. 'Before the invasion, the war was between only you and the Germans – they were in control and you were underground – but now the war's out in the open and your many allies are also involved – British, American, Canadian, Australian, freed Europeans, your fellow Frenchmen – so you can't fight the way you did before, as if you're the only ones. Instead, you must think of what's happening elsewhere and plan according to that.'

'Which means?'

'No more accidental encounters, André. No summary executions. No driving about in the daylight just to find a fire-fight. We have to move under cover of darkness and make our plans carefully. We have to be more precise.'

'He's insulting you!' Maxine hissed.

André looked steadily at her, admiring her fierce courage and conviction. Then he smiled slightly and said: 'No, I think not.' Turning back to Callaghan, he asked: 'You want to take control of my men, Captain?'

'No, I don't think that would help.'

'Why not?'

'I don't think they would take orders from me.'

A sly form of flattery, this made André smile.

'Correct, Captain. They would not take orders from you. If you angered them, they would shoot you in the back and throw your body into a ditch. They have no time for doubts.'

'That I appreciate,' Callaghan informed him. 'You've lived close to the edge.'

'On the edge of a razor,' Maxine told him, 'so we do things our own way.'

Callaghan smiled. 'All right, I'll grant you that. Nevertheless, we have to somehow work together and take the best from each other.'

'Agreed,' André said. 'We have fought too long without support and now we need yours.' Maxine glared at him, but he ignored her. 'What do you propose?'

'We retain the concept of three groups, but instead of the Maquis being divided between the three, they will now form the whole of the third group, operating under your leadership. We will travel by night instead of by day, to avoid accidental confrontations with the enemy; and only hit hard targets that can be taken by surprise.'

'What does that mean?' Maxine asked, her delicate features showing a tightly controlled rage mixed with a grudging interest.

'Railway lines and trains; aircraft and airfields; radar installations and other communications centres; convoys on the move with the troops still in the trucks; FOBs . . .'

'Pardon?' André interjected.

'Forward operating bases or, for the purpose of your attacks, any German bases or camps which, at night, are in a state of relative inactivity and can be attacked with the benefit of surprise.'

'The British have turned cowardice into an art form,' Maxine spat.

Callaghan shrugged and spread his hands in the air as if asking to be pardoned for his sins. 'What can I say? War is war and the loser loses all – and we can't afford that. We have hundreds of thousands of Allied troops advancing through France towards Germany and we can't risk their lives for misplaced feelings of honour. In other words, we do not invite the Germans to shoot us before we fire our own weapons. We do not travel in broad daylight only to run unexpectedly into well-armed German columns. We do not announce our arrival to the enemy and trust they will let us win. This isn't cowardice, *mademoiselle*; it's simple common sense. I trust you will see that.'

There was silence for a moment, then, after glancing at André, Maxine nodded her agreement.

'Good,' Callaghan said. 'Now why don't we pool our information about German strength and movements, about the locations of their most strategically important camps, airstrips or communications centres, and work out a precise plan of attack based on three different groups all attacking in different areas at once?'

'I have everything marked up on these maps,' André said, tugging a handful of maps from the rucksack on his back. 'Let's work out who does what.'

'Excellent,' Callaghan replied, smiling at Greaves and Lorrimer.

By the time the meeting ended, an hour later, each group leader knew what the other group was doing and was prepared to do it.

Even Maxine was pleased.

9

The men had a good rest that night, sleeping in their lean-tos or LUPs hidden by the trees, but they were up at first light the following morning to wash in the nearby stream, have a quick breakfast of cold rations with water, and then organize the temporary camp as a proper FOB. While some of them remained in the camp itself to clean and oil weapons, study maps of the areas, practise their French and check the supplies and vehicles, others were sent out in four different directions to construct observation posts and keep a record of the direction, frequency and size of passing enemy columns and aircraft.

'Every last damn vehicle,' Captain Callaghan warned them. 'Every tank, armoured car, truck, jeep, motor-bike or bicycle. As for the aircraft, I want to know the type – heavy bomber, light bomber, fighter plane, escort – the direction of flight, and the time it was spotted. I want nothing missed nor forgotten. Now get to it, men.'

As they were planning to be there for some time, the men constructed rectangular observation posts, which were deeper and larger than the short-term, diamond-shaped OPs. Facing outwards, away from the camp, the rectangular OP contained four shallow scrapes: one for the observer, one for the sentry, one for the man assigned to keep records and a fourth as a rest bay. A small well was dug in the centre, to drain off excess water such as rain, and the roof was made of chicken wire, camouflage netting and foliage that helped it blend in with its surroundings. The OP had a camouflaged entry cum exit hole and there was a long, thin viewing slit between the upturned earth and the artificial roof in the side that faced away from the camp.

Once constructed, the OP was filled with everything the men would need for long-term observation of both sky and land, including black-painted binoculars and a tripod-mounted telescope, maps, log book, cipher book, camera, S-phone and MCR1 receiver for contact with SAS foot patrols or the FOB, water and rations, sleeping bags for the shallow scrapes, spare batteries and clothing, and personal and close-support weapons, including a Webley pistol, 9mm Sten gun, Thompson M1 sub-machine-gun and two .303-inch Lee-Enfield bolt-action rifles. Thus equipped, the men settled down and began their observation.

At the same time, Captain Callaghan was huddling with Corporal Jim Almonds, giving the squadron's signaller a list of requirements for a resup drop to take place that night. Almonds relayed the request by Morse code over the No. 11 radio set to London, from where it would be passed on to their air-support group at RAF Station 1090, Down Ampney, Gloucestershire. The supplies, which included replacement Willys jeeps for the six lost, would be flown out from there.

While the men were setting up their OPs and Callaghan was contacting London, Greaves was decoding messages received in code from the BBC regarding the progress of the battle for Europe. When the messages were decoded, he was able to tell those gathered around him – Jacko and Rich, Harry-boy and Neil – that since they had parachuted into France a massive Allied invasion force of British, American, Canadian and French troops had started advancing along a 100-mile front from Nice to Marseilles; Paris had been liberated by General Leclerc's French 2nd Armoured Division; American forces were continuing to advance on Reims and Verdun; the British 2nd Army was sweeping across the bridgeheads of the Seine, heading for Amiens; and French troops and General Patton's 3rd Army were racing in from opposite directions to capture Dijon.

'I'll take Paris,' Jacko told his mates when Captain Greaves had departed. 'The rest of those Frog towns you can keep, but Paris should be worth seeing.'

'The way the war's going it should all be over in no time,' Rich informed them, 'so we might get there sooner than you think.'

The four men were sitting in a small circle on the grass, cleaning and oiling their personal weapons.

'We'll probably liberate France pretty soon,' Neil said, 'but we've still got the whole of Germany to cover.'

'The Russians are practically there already,' Jacko told him, 'so that won't take long either. Before you know it, this war's gonna be over and we'll all get leave in France.'

'I don't think *everyone* in the Allied armies can be given leave in France,' Harry-boy put in. 'Too many of us, mate. So I reckon that as soon as the war ends, we'll all be shipped home. No Paris. No French tarts. *Nothing*'

'Or get shipped to Italy,' Rich said solemnly. 'The war's still being fought there.'

'Right,' Neil said. 'But Florence has already fallen to the Allies and the rest of Italy's set to fall.'

'That's 'cause the Eyeties don't like fighting,' Harry-boy said. 'They just like wine, women and song. They don't even care who runs Italy, so long as they can still have a good time. Carefree, that's what they are.'

'Bloody useless Eyeties,' Jacko opined. 'About all they're good for is making pasta and yodelling.'

'They don't yodel,' Rich corrected him. 'They sing opera.'

'Can't understand a word of it, mate, so it sounds like yodelling to me.'

'They aren't as bad as soldiers as people say,' Harry-boy insisted. 'They certainly fought well in Sicily.'

'Fought well?' Jacko repeated in disbelief. 'The only English word they learnt is "surrender" and they used it a lot, mate!'

'Not in Sicily,' Rich said. 'I agree with Harry-boy on that. The Eyeties, they may not be great soldiers, but they did their best down there.'

'They just don't want to die, see?' Harry-boy put in. 'They're philosophical, like, when it comes to being alive, and they think more of the good things of life than they do of fighting wars.'

'They don't believe in dying for their country,' Neil said. 'That's what Harry-boy means when he says they're carefree. You say there's a war on and it's very important and your average Eyetie will reply: "What's important?" They don't know what that means, like.'

'Jesus!' Jacko exclaimed. 'I don't believe my own ears! You bastards are defending the soldiers who're so busy keeping their hands above their heads they can't even wank.'

'Jacko's famous filthy tongue!' Rich said in disgust.

'I'd recommend him to wash it out with iodine,' Neil said, 'but as we know, the bastard could drink anything and get the best out of it.'

'Anyway, we weren't talking about the bloody Eyeties,' Harry-boy said. 'We were talking about the end of the war in Europe and us getting to Paris.'

'Gay Paree!' Neil said, laughing. 'The old in-and-out in Montmartre! What more could a man want?'

They all stared at him, stunned. They hadn't realized he was educated.

'What the fuck's Montmartre?' Jacko asked. 'A Frog *museum* or something?'

'The cancan!' Neil informed him, warming to his theme. 'Women dancing and throwing their skirts above their heads. Music! Nightclubs! Striptease! For Christ's sake, Jacko, don't you know *anything*?'

'You mean you've already *been* there?' Jacko asked, taken aback.

''Course not,' Neil replied, coming back down to earth. 'But I've seen it at the pictures, see – and read all about it. Bloody fantastic place! I mean, Montmartre *is* Paris, for God's sake!'

Caught between monumental relief – the very thought that Moffatt had *already* been to Paris – and bitter disappointment, Jacko rolled his eyes and said with a sneer: 'Well, isn't that a bleedin' revelation? The halfwit thinks Paris is great because he's never been there. I bet it's just another French piss-hole.'

'I thought you wanted to go to Paris,' Rich said. 'In fact, you're the one who started this bloody conversation by saying you wanted to spend your leave in Paris, so why . . .?'

'Fuck all this rubbish about Paris,' Jacko replied rather too quickly. 'What *I* want to know is why we're sitting here on our arses when we could be out doing damage to Jerry.'

'We're waiting to go on a resup collection,' Rich solemnly reminded him.

'Ah, yes!' Jacko said, pretending that he had needed the reminder. 'A soldier's work is never done.'

They were still talking at last light when, just as boredom was setting in, they were called by Sergeant Lorrimer to help out at the night's resup DZ.

Again, Callaghan had picked a drop zone approximately two miles from the camp in case the Germans saw the landing lights. Again, he picked a field nearly 1000 yards long and encircled it with SAS and Maquis armed guards, all facing away from the field, towards where an advancing enemy could be seen. This time, however, instead of brushwood beacons, the DZ was marked with four proper lights, three red and one white, though as usual spread 100 yards apart in an L shape, with the white light at the end of the short leg.

When the distant growling of four powerful Rolls-Royce Merlin engines announced that the Halifax was approaching, Callaghan, using Morse code, flashed clearance to land, but this time using a large signalling lamp instead of a hand torch. Once the Halifax had banked towards the illuminated DZ, Corporal Almonds plugged in the short-directional aerial of his S-phone and used it both as a homing beacon and as a radio-telephone link with the aircraft's pilot for final instructions. At the same time, another group of SAS troopers, including Jacko, Rich, Neil and Harry-boy, ran with their backs to the wind, facing the incoming plane, to take up positions on both sides of the long leg of the DZ, ready to race in and collect the dropped canisters.

When the Halifax was overhead and the mass of crates and canisters floated down on the end of their multiple parachutes, the men carefully avoided being hit by them but rushed to collect them once they had landed in the field. Within minutes the canisters had been opened, emptied and buried, and the men transferred their contents to the waiting trucks.

Even as the trucks were moving away from the DZ, more brilliant-white parachutes billowed up above as the crates containing the replacement jeeps floated down. When the crates were on the ground, the men broke them open, buried the separate pieces of wood, covered the disturbed soil with loose leaves and other foliage, then hurriedly loaded the smaller crates containing the weapons into the jeeps and drove away.

The Halifax turned back the way it had come and disappeared in the dark sky.

'Perfect,' Callaghan whispered. 'Not a German in sight. Let's get out while we can, men.'

The drive back through the dark, wind-blown countryside was uneventful, except for the jagged flashes illuminating the horizon and reminding them that the war was continuing. Once at the FOB, the men gave the new jeeps a thorough mechanical check. When this proved satisfactory, they carefully mounted the twin Vickers .303-inch K guns front and rear and fixed a fifth to the driver's side. Next, they attached the wire-cutter to the armour plating across the front bumper; slotted the bulletproof Perspex screens into place; hooked the reserve fuel tanks under the driver's seat and over the lockers at the back; then packed in as many boxes of spare ammunition as they could – armour-piercing and incendiary bullets, tracer, and rounds of ball ammo – plus water cans, food supplies, flares and an S-phone and Eureka beacon. Modified and fully loaded, the jeeps looked formidable indeed.

Finally, with everything unpacked and prepared for the next day's patrol, the men were allowed to relax and open the most precious boxes of all: the ones containing cigarettes and letters from home. Seated on the ground, either in or near their own bashas, they smoked and read their letters by the light of hand torches pointed downwards, some in silence, others shouting comments back and forth.

'Look at that!' Neil exclaimed. 'Jacko's got two letters from home and he can't even read!'

'I may come from Shoreditch, mate, but I can read and count.'

'Learnt it working on your old man's fruit cart, did you? That only means you can count – probably up to twelve.'

Neil was referring to the fact that Jacko was a true East Ender, who had left school at fourteen and worked for years in Petticoat Lane, selling fruit and vegetables from his father's cart. All of that, of course, was before he enlisted in the Army.

'If I've got two letters,' Jacko said, 'it shows that at least I know people who can write, which is more than we can say for you, Moffatt.'

'Below the belt, Jacko!' Harry-boy exclaimed. 'Just because my mate Neil's from up north doesn't mean he's illiterate. They have schools in Blackburn, you know, and the teachers teach English.'

'Lancashire English!' Jacko replied, speaking and scanning his letters at the same time. 'I don't think that counts, mate. Might as well be a bloody Welshman, coming out with all that garbled Celtic shit.'

'I speak perfect English,' Rich cut in, putting down the letter from his mother, who still lived in their tiny family home in the Welsh coalmining town of Aberfan, where Rich had worked before being called up. 'I just happen to have a very distinctive accent, of which I am proud.'

'The Welsh accent is an abortion,' Harry-boy told him. 'My ears ache when exposed to it.'

'Must be wonderful to come from Islington and learn perfect English from your Paddy neighbours and other working-class foreigners. I stand in awe of your background.'

'Listen, mate, they're bloody good people in Islington, I tell you. At least they speak to each other in English, which is more than the Welsh do.'

'We have our own mother tongue and are proud to speak it. The Welsh are a proud race.'

'I must remember to tell my kids that,' Jacko said, glancing again at one of his letters to learn from his wife's scrawl that his son, Tommy, had just turned six and had a nice party with the in-laws, Tommy's sister, Maggie, who was a year younger, and some neighbours' kids. The party had taken place in the house in Shoreditch, an area full of factories, in the middle of a German air-raid, but that had spoiled no one's fun.

After recounting this little incident to his mates, Jacko said: 'We're a right tough breed down Shoreditch way. It takes a lot to put us off our stride.'

'Not as tough as they are in Aberfan,' Rich told him. 'The coalmines get flooded, escaping gas causes explosions, the tunnels cave in, the dust fills your lungs – but still the men go down there to earn their crust. On top of that, we get bombed night and day by Jerry – so you're not *so* tough in London.'

'I agree,' Neil said. 'I mean, even the women in the cotton mills where I come from . . .'

'Heavenly Blackburn!' Harry-boy interjected.

'. . . are tougher than this lot from the south. About the only thing they're good for in London is shooting their mouths off.'

'That's because we Londoners are literate,' Harry-boy informed him, 'and know how to form complete sentences which, when strung together, actually mean something. Try that with a Welshman or your average halfwit from Lancashire and you'll be wasting your breath.'

'I don't have to listen to this,' Rich said, lighting a cigarette and exhaling a cloud of smoke as he sat back against the tree under which he had made his lean-to. 'I've heard more intelligent conversation between two-year-olds. I'm putting plugs in my ears.'

'Me, too,' Neil said. 'I've been insulted enough for one day. What's worse, I've now got to watch the twat who's insulting me run his fingers along the letters and silently mouth the words he's trying to read. A sight for sore eyes, that is.'

'I've had enough of it myself,' Jacko said, folding up his second letter, then stuffing both letters into the rear pocket of his dispatch rider's breeches. 'I'm going for a piss.'

Adjusting the maroon beret on his head, he moved off at the crouch to find the area designated a common latrine – in the bushes about 200 yards away and about 100 yards behind the men keeping watch out on point. As Jacko disappeared around the far end of the segregated Maquis bell tents – only the SAS slept in LUPs and lean-tos – a distant thunder was heard and the dark horizon was illuminated by a series of silvery-white flashes that appeared to be a hundred miles long.

'Twenty-five pounders,' Harry-boy said.

'Yeah,' Rich agreed. 'But firing across a very broad front, covering half the bloody country.'

'That must mean another push by the Allies advancing on Sombernon, to the west of Dijon. Glad I'm not there, lads.'

'Bloody right,' Neil said. 'A barrage like that can drive you nuts if it doesn't actually kill you. At least we don't have to deal with that.'

'I wouldn't like to be back in Blighty either,' Harry-boy said, squinting as he studied his letter from home by the light of his torch. 'According to what my mum says, Jerry's started dropping his new V-2 rocket bombs. Not nice, she says. Blowing London to hell.'

'They sometimes get it worse than we do, true enough,' Neil told him. 'The Home Front suffers as well.'

'I don't bloody well believe it,' Jacko said, returning at the crouch as the relentless Allied bombardment filled the air with muffled thunder and illuminated the dark horizon with jagged sheets of silvery light.

'Don't believe what?' Harry-boy asked him.

'That fucking Maquis leader, André,' Jacko said, slipping into his shallow LUP, 'and that sweet-faced, murderous little minx.'

'What about 'em?' Neil asked.

'Going at it like dogs in the street,' Jacko explained, outraged. 'They were doing it in André's bell tent and making no bones about it. All yelps and groans. The tent's actually shaking!'

'You're kidding!' Rich exclaimed.

'No, I'm not, mate. They're going at it like two pigs in a trough and making twice as much noise.'

The other three soldiers stared automatically at the bell tents, but they were too far away for any sounds to reach them.

'They're really doing it?' Rich asked, hardly able to credit it, and beginning to colour up.

'Bouncing away like they're on a trampoline,' Jacko confirmed, enjoying Rich's embarrassment, 'and not being remotely quiet about it.'

'Well, I never!' Rich muttered.

'That's the French for you,' Neil told them. 'That's why I want to get to Paris – those Parisian girls are easy.'

'Not that again!' Jacko protested. 'Not more talk about bleedin' Paris. If I hear one more word about Paris I'm gonna throw up.'

'You haven't time,' Harry-boy informed him. 'It's our shift on guard.'

'Already?' Rich asked, checking his illuminated wristwatch. 'Christ, yes, you're right! Let's get up and go.'

Wearily, the men all emerged from their respective LUPs or lean-tos, carrying their personal weapons – a 9mm Sten gun for Jacko, a tommy-gun for Rich and .303-inch Lee-Enfield bolt-action assault rifles for Neil and Harry-boy – and made their way to their separate points to replace the men already there. Lying in carefully concealed scrapes, they spent the next four hours staring at the dark fields and forest straight ahead and at the flashes on the distant horizon. Not able to see each other, peering into the darkness, they spent a tense, lonely vigil, during which they could not relax for a minute. They did, however, ease their loneliness and tension by thinking of various things even as they kept their eyes peeled and their other senses alert.

Jacko thought of his wife and kids in Shoreditch, surprised at how little he missed them. He then dwelt on the more exciting times he had had with the Long Range Desert Group in North Africa just over three years ago. He also thought of the many different women he had had – both before and since his marriage – and started imagining the kind he would meet if he ever got to Paris – women like that bitch Maxine, the very sight of whom gave him an erection. Normally, however, Jacko liked unsophisticated women with big tits and a subservient nature. He figured he might find that kind in Paris and the possibility was exciting. The thought that he was betraying his wife never entered his head.

Harry-boy distracted himself with more mundane recollections of his home off Islington's Caledonian Road, where, when not with the Army, he still lived with his parents. His father was a driver for a local furniture store and even now Harry-boy could only look back with unalloyed pleasure on the many days he had bunked off school and helped his dad deliver anything from a footstool to a three-piece suite on his rounds all over north London. He also thought of his girlfriend, Linda, from just up the road in Holloway. She had once wanted to marry him, but had since sent him a letter saying that since she hadn't seen him since 1941, when he had put off marrying her, she was now getting engaged to someone else. Despite the fact that what she had said was correct, Harry-boy burned up with humiliation and anger each time he thought of that letter. Nevertheless, it was the humiliation and rage that kept him alert throughout his long vigil.

Rich thought a lot about his early days in Aberfan, where he had been a miner. Though life was hard, the people were good and the community spirit a great comfort. For that very reason Rich had not wanted to join the Army and had resented being conscripted, but since being accepted by L Detachment in 1941, he had come to love being a soldier and now knew he would never go down the mines again. Nevertheless, when he felt lonely, he took comfort from thoughts of Aberfan and its close-knit community. You didn't have that kind of life in London, no matter what Jacko said; it was more impersonal there. So Rich took a lot of comfort during his lonely vigil by thinking of home. He hadn't been back there for five years, but it still lived inside him.

Neil, on the other hand, had few fond memories of his childhood and youth in Blackburn. Contrary to what he had told Jacko, he'd had a miserable upbringing both at school and, later, when he had become an apprentice textile machinist in one of Blackburn's largest cotton mills. Neil's father and mother between them had run a small electrical goods business in the centre of town and made Neil work there at weekends, even when he was still at school. For that reason, he had not had much spare time to spend with his school chums and, by the time he left school, at fourteen, and went into the cotton mill, he had very few friends left. Perhaps it was his feelings of loneliness that made him sign up with the Territorial Army in his local drill hall in 1939; certainly, once in the TA, he had found the kind of camaraderie he had lacked throughout his childhood and it had brought him out of himself a little. Within months of joining the TA, which he attended at weekends, he had become involved with a girl, Florence, from the cotton mill, with whom he had had many sweaty evenings that had not led to sex. Indeed, he still hadn't been to bed with Florence eighteen months later, when he transferred from the TA to the regular Army and was shipped to North Africa. Now, proud to be one of the Originals of L Detachment, and now a member of 1 SAS Brigade, he wasn't sure if he actually loved his plump Florence, though he certainly thought a lot about her and burned up at the thought of touching her large, bare breasts, which is all she had ever let him do. Those thoughts, though sometimes giving him an erection, also managed to keep him alert throughout his lonely vigil.

Jacko, Harry-boy, Rich and Neil were relatively lucky. Their shift on point was from midnight to four in the morning, which meant that they could catch three hours' sleep before, at first light, they had to rise again, have a quick breakfast, and then spend the rest of the day on foot patrol, reconnoitring the area, checking the local farms for German troops and marking points of strategic interest on their route maps.

They were, however, only relatively lucky, for that long, hot, exhausting day was not followed by another period of rest. Instead, at 2200 hours, as planned, all the men were ordered into the jeeps and moved out in three separate columns for the first of their night raids.

10

The three separate groups moved out at thirty-minute intervals, with Group One, led by Captain Callaghan, following the road south, Group Two, led by Captain Greaves, forking off to the east, and Group Three, the Maquis group headed by André, branching off to the west.

The two SAS groups were strung out as they would have been in single file on foot patrol: the jeep containing Sergeant Lorrimer, Jacko and Rich was up at the front on point, constantly checking what lay ahead. The jeep containing Captain Greaves, Harry-boy Turnball and Neil Moffatt was second in line, followed by the radio jeep, manned by Sergeant Pat Riley, Corporal Jim Almonds and Corporal Benny Bennett, then three other jeeps. Finally, the seventh jeep, manned by Sergeants Bob Tappman and Ernie Bond, with Corporal Reg Seekings driving, was acting as 'Tail-end Charlie'.

Being out on point, the job of the gunners in the first jeep was to cover an arc-shaped area of fire in front of the column. The jeeps in the middle not only protected the radio jeep, but covered arcs to left and right. Those in the last jeep had to constantly swing around to face the direction from which they had come, not only covering the column's rear but also ensuring that the patrol had no blind spots. Given that in some way or another every man in the column had to constantly look for signs of enemy movement, either on the road ahead, on the road behind or in the fields on either side, as well as check repeatedly that the jeeps front and rear were still in place, the watch routines were emotionally and physically demanding, often leading to a great deal of tension and eventual exhaustion. Nevertheless they could not be ignored.

The column travelled into the darkness along a lane that wound like a snake and often appeared to curve back on itself, though in fact it passed through hamlets of white-roofed cottages, small fields of crops, hedges and gently undulating hills. In daylight, they would have had to drive very slowly to avoid throwing up a tell-tale dust cloud, but in the early morning darkness there was no such risk and they could travel as fast as they pleased, which was as fast as the narrow roads and sharp bends permitted.

Eventually, after a couple of hours, during which nothing was seen, the lane came to a dead end at a gate leading into a farm. Immensely frustrated, and to moans and groans from the men in the other jeeps, the column had to reverse back along the lane until the last jeep came parallel to a track that cut across the dark fields. The whole column reversed past the track until the first jeep could turn into it; the others then followed, which kept them in the same order as before. They then travelled across the fields, along what was no more than a narrow dried-mud track filled with potholes and mounds, making the jeeps bounce up and down constantly as they passed herds of cows and sheep.

After about an hour of this, during which they seemed to have travelled hardly any distance at all, they were further frustrated when they came to a fast-running stream about six feet wide. Luckily, when Sergeant Lorrimer got out to check the depth of the water and the consistency of the bed with a stick, the water was only ten inches deep at its deepest and the bottom was mostly gravel on compacted earth. The jeeps were therefore able to cross by inching slowly down the bank and into the water, then moving through the stream even more slowly and revving dramatically to get up the other bank and back on to the track.

When the radio jeep, the heaviest vehicle, sank into a patch of mud in the middle of the stream, Corporals Almonds and Benny Bennett lightened the load by clambering out and taking a lot of the gear with them; then, with Sergeant Pat Riley at the steering wheel, the mud was scraped away from under the wheels, steel sand channels were shoved under them, separating them from the bed, and the jeep, with its engine running in low gear, was pushed out by the soaked, cursing Almonds and Bennett. Once the wheels were free of the mud, Riley gunned the engine and the jeep screeched up the far bank, following the others.

From there, they took an even more unpredictable and narrow track across country, using the wire-cutters fixed on the front armour plating of the jeep to break through the many wire or barbed-wire fences, as well as to hack through the many hedges they encountered. In this way they came eventually to what was, according to their maps, the village of Jeux, and drove as quietly as possible into its darkened, deserted main street.

Not quite deserted. They were, in fact, all taken by surprise when the door of the village bistro opened a little, shedding light briefly into the darkness, and an obviously drunken French farmer emerged. Seeing him, Sergeant Lorrimer stopped his jeep, then used a hand signal to stop the column behind him. Then, while the Frenchman, though drunk, stopped and stared in growing surprise at the column of 'liberators', Lorrimer glanced quizzically over his shoulder at Captain Greaves, whose jeep had braked to a rapid halt, almost hitting his own. Greaves nodded his agreement, then spoke in French to the farmer.

'Good morning, *monsieur*.'

The farmer hiccuped, then managed: 'Good morning. English, yes?'

'Yes.'

'We have already been liberated, which is why . . .' The farmer hiccuped again, then smiled benignly and spread his hands in the air as if praying to God for forgiveness. 'Which is why I am drunk, *monsieur*. The whole village has had an evening of wine and calvados. That place behind me . . .' – he indicated the closed door of the bistro – '. . . is still packed with villagers.'

Greaves and the others could now hear laughter and singing from within. The captain grinned at the Frenchman. 'Yes, I understand, *monsieur*. These are good days for all of us.'

The Frenchman hiccuped. 'Good days. We've waited a long time for this. It is good to see you and those who came before you. But tell me, what are you doing here at this time of night – or rather morning?'

'We're looking for Germans.'

'Ah! Yes! Very good!' The Frenchman placed his index finger to his nose, then used the same finger to point beyond the town. 'A whole Panzer division without its tanks – I mean, a division of Panzer troops – is. strung out right across this area, though mainly between Semur and Montard. What are such troops without tanks? Go after them, Captain!'

'We will.'

The Frenchman hiccuped again and winked. 'Annihilate them, Captain. Get rid of them. Exterminate them like the vile scum they are.'

'We will,' Captain Greaves promised.

In fact, he had no such intention. An open conflict with such a sizeable company could only have led to disaster and Greaves had other fish to fry. Nevertheless, it was diplomatic to let the Frenchman think otherwise – his story of this encounter would doubtless resound throughout the village tomorrow. In the meantime, Greaves felt it expedient to go on to more realistic matters.

With Sergeant Lorrimer's jeep out on point, the SAS column drove on into the night, making a wide detour around the estimated location of the German Panzer division to avoid a damaging conflict with them. Before long, however, the lane they were driving along turned into a bewildering maze of cart tracks that soon had them driving in circles, only knowing that they were east of the main road. Attempting to get back to it, they found themselves bouncing roughly over a ploughed field that led them to the summit of a hill overlooking the very road they were trying to find. As all of the jeeps, one after the other, came abreast on the summit, the whole squadron found themselves looking down at the moving headlights of a German convoy of trucks passing right by them.

Immediately, they switched off their engines and sat in complete silence, waiting until the last truck had passed. Then they drove down the winding track to the same road and headed off in the opposite direction, taking the first side road that led in the direction marked on their route maps. Eventually, about three in the morning, they arrived at a closed level crossing at the foot of a sharp incline. Before there was time to withdraw the jeeps, they heard the sound of a train coming round the shoulder of the hill. The chugging gradually became louder until they were able to see that it was a goods train of about twenty wagons, boldly flying a large swastika, and still about half a mile down the track.

Lorrimer instantly switched on his S-phone and contacted Greaves, telling him the situation and adding: 'It's too good to resist, boss.'

'I agree,' Greaves said. 'I want the jeeps to spread out into the fields on both sides of the road, covering both sides of that level crossing. At my signal – which will be when the train is exactly halfway across the crossing – we'll open fire on it with everything we've got, including the mortar. Convey that order to the men, Sergeant.'

'Yes, boss,' Lorrimer said. Still using his S-phone, Lorrimer passed the order down the line. The jeeps, in single file, pulled around each other and, in most cases, bounced off the road until they were forming a long line parallel to the railway track, on both sides of the level crossing. Once in position, the gunners, not including the drivers, cocked their Vickers K guns and prepared to fire. As they were doing so, the mortar team jumped out of their jeep, quickly dug a shallow hole for the steel base plate, buried it, packed it tight with shells, and then fixed the mortar to the base plate and looked towards Greaves.

When the train reached the gates of the level crossing, Greaves raised his right hand.

When the train had passed the gates and the line of transport carriages was halfway across – when, in fact, the German machine-gun crews on the open platforms were clearly visible in moonlight – Greaves dropped his hand abruptly.

Instantly, the mortar sent its shell in a great arc towards the track just in front of the engine. Even as the shell exploded with a startling roar, hurling up twisted metal, lumps of wood, soil and gravel in a billowing cloud of smoke, causing the driver to apply the brakes and the locked wheels to screech, the massed Vickers opened up, pouring streams of mixed incendiary, tracer and armour-piercing bullets into the whole length of the train, including the open platforms bearing the German machine-gun crews.

It was a spectacular sight. Before the German troops knew what had hit them, the train became a bizarre carnival of criss-crossing lines of green tracer, spitting flames, billowing smoke and exploding splinters of wood. The German machine-gun crews on the open platforms were torn apart with shocking speed and ferocity, with men screaming, throwing their hands up, then either jerking violently and collapsing around their weapons or falling off the edge of the still-moving train, to bounce brutally down the sides of the track, through loose gravel and clouds of sand.

The engine was unharmed by the first mortar shell, but the second explosion tore the tracks up right in front of it, derailing it and causing it to plunge down into the field, dragging the carriages with it. Then, like a giant accordion played by a mad musician, the carriages smashed into one another, rising up like a pyramid, then crashing back down in a dreadful tangle of steel, wood and exploding glass. Finally, even before the carriages had collapsed back on to the track, ammunition and petrol exploded, creating a dazzling fireworks display that included great jagged fans of flame and clouds of oily, black smoke. The carriages, including those carrying the German machine-gun crews, then rolled over sideways and went crashing down into the fields. The engine, already lying in the field under the SAS troops, pouring clouds of hissing, scalding steam, suddenly exploded into a scorching ball of fire that set fire to the branches of the nearest trees.

Even as the few surviving enemy troops were fleeing up into the woods at the other side of the track, ignoring the demented screaming of their burning, dying comrades, the SAS jeeps stopped firing, rolled across the track and continued south as fast as they possibly could, losing themselves in a darkness illuminated by the flames of the burning train.

Again, when they drove on, the SAS men came into no direct contact with German foot patrols or armoured columns. Indeed, they were beginning to believe that they were on a wasted journey when they reached the edge of the Forest of Chantillon. There, the jeep out on point stopped and its lights went off. Seeing this, Greaves told his own driver, Neil Moffatt, to do the same. When Moffatt had done so, Greaves used a hand signal to tell the rest of the column to follow suit.

Eventually, when the column was silent and still, hidden in moonlit darkness, Lorrimer came running back from his jeep, still out on point, to report that there was a German radar station in a clearing just beyond the trees.

Even as he was speaking, a number of German machine-guns opened fire on the jeeps.

The SAS gunners returned the fire with their Vickers as the drivers throttled the engines and drove the jeeps to opposite sides of the road, practically burying their armoured bumpers in the tall hedgerows. From there, though unable to see where the German fire was coming from, the gunners sprayed the undergrowth ahead, tearing it to shreds, as if devastated by a hellish tornado.

'Enemy still unseen,' Lorrimer, still out front, conveyed to Greaves over the S-phone. 'We're still firing blind and without adequate protection. We could get chopped to pieces.'

'Everyone withdraw!' Greaves snapped into the open line. 'Stop when I say so.'

The Tail-end Charlie jeep instantly went into reverse, screeched into a three-point turn in the narrow lane and headed back the way it had come, leaving a swirling cloud of dust behind it. The other jeeps did the same, one after the other, until they were all heading back around the first bend in the road, about a mile away. Now second-to-last in line, Greaves waited until he knew that the final jeep, containing Lorrimer, Jacko and Rich, was safely around the bend and out of sight, before he snapped 'Stop!' into the S-phone. The jeeps then all screeched to a halt, still in a column but facing back the way they had come. At another instruction from Greaves, they drove closer to one another, until they were bunched dangerously close together. Greaves only permitted this because he intended going back to attack the Germans before they had the chance to pursue him.

'The Chantillon radar station,' he said to Harry-boy and their driver, Neil Moffatt. 'It's not clearly marked on the map, but there's a separate reference to it.'

'Terrific,' Harry-boy said sarcastically.

'Jesus,' Neil added. 'That means we're close to the front. Those Krauts must have mistaken us for the advance guard of the US 3rd Army.'

'Very likely,' Greaves told him. He thought for a moment, studying the map, then shrugged, grinned in an oddly shy manner, and said: 'Well, if they're already worried, let's give them something real to worry about.'

On instructions conveyed by Greaves on the S-phone, one man remained in each jeep, manning a Vickers, while the others climbed down, carrying their personal and some heavy weapons, and clambered through or over the hedges, depending on the density of the foliage, to make their way as silently as possible along the edge of the field, back to the vicinity of the radar station.

It was well before dawn, so the morning was still dark, but in the moonlight the SAS men could clearly see the bunker-shaped buildings of the radar station. The whole area was surrounded by barbed wire and machine-guns posts, and the station was dominated by a central control tower etched like a black finger against the pale moon.

'Piece of piss,' Jacko whispered. 'That control tower's as visible as my hard-on when I'm having a shower.'

'Modest as always,' Rich replied. 'So how the hell do we get to it?'

'The three-inch mortar,' Lorrimer told him, then made the same recommendation to Greaves over the S-phone.

'Agreed,' the captain said. 'But before we blow the tower, I think we should call up reinforcements to enable us to put out the whole radar station when the tower is down.'

'Right, boss. Captain Callaghan?'

'Yes. Get in touch with him. Once we know they're on the way, we'll blow the control tower. That should encourage some of the Krauts to evacuate and leave us less to tackle when the CO and his men get here. Agreed, Sergeant?'

'I'm with you all the way, boss.' Using his S-phone, Lorrimer conveyed Greaves's instructions to Corporal Jim Almonds. When the signaller had conveyed the message by Morse code via the No. 11 radio set and received coded confirmation back, Lorrimer called up the mortar crew.

The two men emerged from the moonlit darkness of the lane, quickly embedded the metal base plate in the earth near the hedgerow, set up the mortar, made a visual estimation of the alignment and awaited the signal to fire. When Lorrimer, at a nod from Greaves, dropped his raised right hand, the first shell was fired.

The minor explosion of the firing mortar was followed almost immediately by the much louder noise of the exploding shell, which tore up soil and loose gravel in a cloud of smoke just short of the radar station's control tower. Instantly, without knowing where they were firing, the German sentries opened up with their machine-guns, spraying a wide arc of fire over the road around the bend, well out of range, and out of the sight, of the SAS column. Nevertheless, the combined noise of the exploding mortar and machine-guns was deafening.

Having used the first mortar shot purely as a visual reference, the mortar crew adjusted the calibration and fired a second shell. It exploded with a mighty roar just beyond the control tower, showering it in a downfall of swirling soil and loose gravel, before obscuring it in billowing clouds of smoke.

Splitting the difference between the first and second visual sightings, the mortar crew fired their third shell and were gratified to see the tower take a direct hit. Its pagoda-style wooden roof was blown off entirely, the struts beneath it split and buckled, then the whole of the top half blew apart, the machine-gun crew spilling out and screaming dreadfully as they fell to earth. A fourth and fifth mortar shell, fired one right after the other, virtually demolished the tower and made it collapse, sending crimson sparks showering up from the blazing wood to illuminate the dark, moonlit sky.

Even as this was happening, the gates of the radar station were opening to let heavily armed, helmeted German troops race out, some sheltering to the left of the lane, others to the right. On both sides they advanced, firing blindly from the hip, but with a potentially devastating amount of fire-power.

'*Retreat*!' Greaves bawled into his S-phone.

Instantly, the SAS men on the ground returned to their jeeps and, now facing away from the tower, were driven away from the German troops and out of range in a matter of seconds. However, under telephoned instructions from Greaves, they kept going for thirty minutes until they reached the next village. Knowing that the Germans would not follow them this far, but would return to the radar station, either to evacuate or regroup for a defensive action, the SAS men disembarked from the jeeps and relaxed with cigarettes and drinks of cold water from their flasks, waiting for Callaghan to arrive with the reinforcements.

The CO's column of seven jeeps arrived at the village just before first light. Noting that Greaves's men were lolling about the village square at dawn, inviting the curiosity of the surprised, sleepy villagers and clearly enjoying their cold breakfast, Callaghan grinned broadly as he approached his second in command.

'I thought you men were having a hard time,' he said, 'but this looks like a party.'

'Not quite,' Greaves replied good-humouredly. 'What we have along the road is a German radar station that's lost its control tower but still has a bunch of crack troops defending it. I suspect that the loss of the tower will encourage them to evacuate, but I say we should go and attack while we still have the advantage.'

'If we do, we must do it right now,' Callaghan insisted, 'before they move out.'

'Ready, willing and able.'

The two groups of jeeps moved out of the village and, as quickly as the lane would allow, headed back to the radar station. The flames of the destroyed control tower had flickered out by the time they reached their destination, but it was now light enough to see the lazily rising smoke from the smouldering wreckage around the sharp curve in the lane. Not knowing what lay around that bend, but assuming that the German troops would have retreated back into the barbed-wire enclosure of the radar station, some of the SAS men jumped down from the jeeps, leaving a driver and one gunner in each vehicle. Splitting into two groups, one on either side of the road, both hugging the hedgerows, they marched quietly, cautiously around the bend with their personal weapons at the ready.

As Greaves had suspected, the Germans had retreated from the lane, back into the barbed-wire compound, and were evacuating the radar station, via the rear gate, in troop trucks, jeeps and armoured cars and on foot, under the protection of gunners whose machine-guns were aimed in the opposite direction, towards the bend and the SAS troops it was concealing.

'If we advance any further,' Lorrimer whispered to Callaghan and Greaves. 'We'll be chopped to pieces.'

'A few mortar shells should do the job nicely,' Callaghan suggested with a devilish smile. 'What say you, Dirk?'

'Absolute agreement, old boy,' Greaves replied. 'Lob 'em in and let's go.'

While the bulk of the men knelt on each side of the road, hugging the hedgerows, the mortar team went just around the bend, where they set up the mortar. Their immediate priority was the machine-gun crews defending the main gate, one on either side; their second was the other machine-gun crews along the front barbed-wire fence. This time, having already ascertained the correct calibrations from their attack on the control tower, they were able to drop their first mortar shells almost directly on the gate, between the machine-gun teams on either side. The resultant blast not only split the night's silence with a deafening roar, but blew the barrier of the gatehouse to pieces and showered both machine-gun emplacements with debris from the building, and with soil and gravel.

Unharmed, the German machine-gunners on either side of the barrier opened fire ferociously, turning the road in front of the SAS mortar crew, as well as the hedges on either side of them, into a tornado of leaves, branches and dust. Undeterred, the mortar crew made adjustments to their line of fire and fired two more shells, one to the left, one to the right, tearing up the ground just in front of one gun emplacement and blowing another up entirely. Beyond curtains of swirling smoke, they could just make out Germans screaming and writhing spectrally in the chaos.

'Very nice,' Callaghan murmured. 'But not quite enough. I want those other gun positions destroyed before the men are asked to advance. Sergeant?'

'Yes, boss,' Lorrimer said. Disappearing around the bend, he returned a few minutes later and said: 'Keep your fingers crossed, boss.'

Callaghan and Greaves's position in the road just about allowed them to see around the bend without exposing themselves to enemy fire. Their ears came into play when they heard three mortar shells exploding, one after the other in quick succession. Then, when they witnessed the exploding gun emplacements, and heard the enemy soldiers screaming as they somersaulted and crashed back down to earth, they had seen enough to let them simultaneously call out: 'Attack!'

Naturally courageous, but unerringly cautious, the SAS men advanced at the crouch around the bend, hugging their respective hedgerows at both sides of the road. Then, seeing that the Germans' front gun emplacements had indeed been demolished, they released themselves from their constraints and raced pell-mell towards the demolished main gates. Isolated bursts of rifle and machine-gun fire from inside the radar station cut some of them down, but as the majority of the Germans were fleeing through the rear gate, most of the SAS managed to surge into the compound at the front.

Once the foot soldiers were inside, the drivers of the jeeps gunned the engines and raced around the bend with the gunners all set to fire. This the gunners did the second they saw their first targets inside the breached compound, adding the savage roar of the twin Vickers to the already deafening cacophony of assault rifles and sub-machine-guns. Thus, while the majority of the Germans had already made their escape, those still inside the compound, some on foot, others in trucks, were cut down in a hail of bullets.

Five minutes later, the mopping up had been completed and the compound was littered with dead bodies. Smoke wreathed the scene of devastation. After checking who was dead and who merely wounded, the SAS picked up their own dead, who numbered five, placed them in the back seats of their jeeps and drove away from the hellish scene, back to the forward operating base.

Once back at the FOB, they arranged for the dead and wounded to be transferred by truck to the nearest Allied airfield; then they all followed breakfast with a long, much-needed sleep. For they knew that by nightfall they would be on the move again, looking for more targets.

11

'I have to confess to being pleased with our progress so far,' Captain Callaghan told Greaves as they watched the Bedford QL trucks rumble out of the FOB, taking more SAS dead away for burial and the wounded to the nearest field hospital, for treatment there or to be casualty-evacuated to England. 'It's astonishing, when you think of it, just how much territory we've covered between us and how many Germans and targets we've managed to knock out during this first fortnight. I can hardly believe it, but it's certainly encouraging.'

'Good for the men's morale as well,' Greaves reminded him.

'Of course.' Glancing about him in the growing light, Callaghan saw that most of the men had finished breakfast and were already creeping into the lean-tos or LUPs for a well-earned kip after the latest of their successful night raids. 'I wonder how the Maquis group's getting on. We haven't heard a peep out of them.'

'Extraordinary,' Greaves said. For the past two weeks, ever since that first night a month ago when they had split up into three separate groups, sending the Maquis out on their own, they hadn't received a single message from André.

To all intents and purposes, the resistance fighters had disappeared like a puff of smoke.

It had been an extraordinary two weeks for more than one reason. In that hectic time, C Squadron had criss-crossed central France relentlessly, always travelling by night, to engage the enemy directly, blow up railway lines, radar stations and communications cables, attack passing trains and troop convoys, and in general cause a great deal of mayhem. In doing so, they had seen a France less welcoming than the one they had experienced during their first, daylight forays across the attractive, mostly liberated countryside. Instead, in the course of their night raids, as the Allies pushed the Germans back towards their own border and the SAS had moved ever closer to the receding front, they had seen the real devastation caused during the occupation and by the retreating Germans since then: whole villages razed to the ground by shelling; churches gutted by fire, with blackened corpses still lying amid their ruins; captured enemy soldiers hanging from trees and lampposts; the bloated, scorched, dismembered carcasses of cows, sheep and horses caught in the cross-fire of battles or misguided bombing raids; rubble, dust and, everywhere, dead soldiers and civilians. During their first two weeks of night raids, the SAS had seen it all.

During that time, also, the war of liberation had continued. The British 2nd Army had advanced 250 miles from the Seine to Antwerp in one week; the 1st Canadian Army had freed Rouen and pushed on to the Somme at Abbeville; Nice and Monaco had been occupied by the Allied forces, who had pushed back the German 19th Army; and General Patton's 3rd Army had reached the north-west edge of Sombernon, on the last leg of its relentless advance to Dijon. The SAS raids in that area were still designed to aid Patton's advance and had so far been very successful.

'Successful though we've been,' Greaves said, 'we've had heavy casualties and I'm worried about our depleted numbers. We're down to half the men and jeeps we had two weeks ago; and according to HQ, we won't be getting any more after the next resup.'

'No problem,' Callaghan replied, grinning broadly. 'Come with me. I've something to show you. It won't take long.'

'I haven't had my morning's sleep yet,' Greaves reminded his fellow captain.

'You can catch up on that later.'

He led Greaves to his jeep and they drove out of the FOB and along the winding lane they had taken so often on their night raids of the past fortnight. Now, in broad daylight, the countryside looked very pretty, with the bright-green, gently undulating hills covered with trees and the occasional white-roofed farmhouse silhouetted against the blue September sky, with its fleecy clouds. This time, however, instead of following the road, Callaghan took a very narrow turning, no more than a dirt track, that led them across a cultivated field and into dense woods.

Eventually, when the trees had become more numerous, cutting down the light, they emerged into a sunlit clearing where, to his surprise, Greaves saw another camp of lean-tos and bell tents concealed cunningly in the trees. As most of the men were wearing Denison smocks, dispatch rider's breeches, motorcycle boots and red berets with the winged-dagger badge, he knew they were members of the SAS.

'D Squadron,' Callaghan explained, pulling up in the middle of the camp, between a row of bell tents and a larger, open-ended tent obviously serving as an HQ. The latter was presently occupied by two officers seated on folding chairs at a trestle-table strewn with maps and papers. 'They parachuted in about a month before us, but in the area of Le Mans. They fought their way from there to Fontainebleau, then moved south to here. I think we can do something about our depleted numbers by joining up with them. So let's meet the CO.'

As they walked across the clearing to the HQ tent, Greaves had a good look around him and was impressed by what he saw: dumps of stores, tents made from khaki parachutes draped between the branches, and brushwood barriers protecting the main exits. Those rude shelters, he realized, would be next to impossible to detect except at the shortest range; and inside, he noticed, they were furnished comfortably with proper camp-beds, folding chairs, small trestle-tables containing hand basins, lamps and hexamine stoves. Very well equipped indeed, Greaves thought. He also noticed that most of the men were bearded and that their berets were beginning to fade. Clearly, they had been out and about a lot.

In the HQ tent the officers, both SAS captains, were still seated at the overburdened trestle-table. Though it was only ten in the morning, one of them, Captain Wilfred 'Will' Lazenby, whom Greaves knew from the SAS camp in Fairford, was filling two glasses with whisky. He looked up when Callaghan and Greaves entered.

'Ah!' he exclaimed. 'We'll need two more glasses.'

'At this time of the morning?' Callaghan asked with mock severity.

Lazenby merely grinned. 'This is D Squadron, not C,' he said. 'We're not softies here. Pull up a chair, Paddy. You, too, Dirk.'

Callaghan and Greaves shook hands with Lazenby, who indicated the other officer with a lazy wave of his free hand. 'Captain Julian Crittenden,' he said. 'A good officer with a mouthful of a name, so just call him Jules.' Greaves shook hands with Crittenden, then pulled up a chair beside Callaghan and accepted the glass of whisky offered by Lazenby. They all raised their glasses in a mock toast, then took the first sip.

'Wonderful!' Lazenby exclaimed softly, reverently. 'This is better than breakfast.'

'Not bad at all,' Callaghan told him. 'You don't go short of anything here, I see.'

'Judging by the look of this place,' Greaves added, 'you've been here some time and are well supplied.'

'Our brief was to avoid engagement with the enemy and instead remain in hiding and concentrate on building up supply dumps in the forest, to be used by the advancing Allies when required. In order to do this we secured an old civilian lorry and used it to transfer the stores from the DZ to various caches scattered widely around the area. Though we did indeed build up a lot of dumps for the advancing troops, we also amassed considerable quantities of food, petrol and ammunition for ourselves – so, yes, we're well stocked and equipped. Now, what have *you* been up to, gentlemen?'

Callaghan summarized the past fortnight's activities, then said: 'So both our SAS groups did extremely well. Unfortunately, we can't tell you how the Maquis group got on as they disappeared and haven't been in touch. Not one radio message.'

'Possibly wiped out by Jerry,' Greaves suggested.

'No, they weren't,' Lazenby said, surprising them both. 'You're talking about the group led by André Flaubert, I take it?'

'Yes.'

'We've been in close contact with that group for the past fortnight,' Lazenby informed them. 'They're presently located at Aignay-le-Duc, about fifteen miles to the south, and they go out daily on hit-and-run raids.'

'By "daily" do you mean during the day?' asked Callaghan.

'Yes. Sometimes at night as well, but mostly during the day. I think they just go when the mood takes them – or when their intelligence informs them of a good target.'

'When you say you've been in close contact,' said Greaves, 'does that mean you're working with them?'

'No. What it means is that we visit them almost every day for information, but otherwise let them do things their own way, which, let's face it, isn't our way.'

'Although the partisans are undoubtedly an enthusiastic bunch,' Crittenden clarified, 'we've found that the difference between our respective methods makes close co-operation difficult. It's therefore better to maintain no more than a loose liaison with them. Isn't that what you found?'

Callaghan sighed and took another sip of whisky. 'Yes. I just wish they'd told us where they were and what they were up to.'

'That's not Flaubert's way. He likes to go his own way.'

'Which is energetic, but completely undisciplined.'

'Quite so, Paddy. And his girlfriend, who has a sweet face, likes to slit German throats.'

'And shoot them in the back of the head,' Greaves informed him.

Lazenby and Crittenden grinned. 'The abrupt dispatch of unhelpful prisoners,' the latter said. 'I think that's a less crude way of putting it.'

Greaves nodded and smiled sardonically. 'Much more tasteful,' he said.

'Are you still in concealment and supplying the dumps?' Callaghan asked.

'No. All that ended last week, when we were told to embark on aggressive patrolling. So a few days ago we began our first offensive moves against Jerry, destroying a number of vehicles, attacking a small post on the main road, blowing up railway lines and bringing down electric pylons with Lewes bombs.'

'God bless Jock Lewes,' Callaghan said and meant it, recalling his late friend with real affection. Lieutenant John Steel Lewes, No. 8 Commando and one of the founder members of the SAS, had created many of the early SAS training methods, invented the highly effective, portable Lewes bomb, and was killed during the raid on Nofilia, in Libya, in December 1941 – shot by an Italian Savoya SM Sparviero light bomber that attacked his LRDG Chevrolet truck. Lewes was now revered by the whole regiment, including Callaghan, who had been on the raid against El Agheila at the same time and marched out of the desert with the other survivors, including Dirk Greaves and David Stirling. He would never forget those raids as long as he lived. He would always miss Lewes.

'God bless Lewes indeed,' Lazenby said. 'Anyway, our activities were pretty successful – certainly enough to encourage a number of countermoves by the Krauts. In fact, they picketed the road between Auberive and Aubepierre and, according to Maquis intelligence, are now beating the forest north of this base, vainly trying to find us.'

'They'll get here eventually,' Callaghan said, 'so you'd better move on.'

'Yes, I suppose so,' Lazenby replied, sighing, 'though I *do* like it here.'

'Since you're going to have to move anyway,' Callaghan said, seeing his chance and taking it, 'why not double your strength by combining with us?'

'Double *your* strength, you mean!'

Callaghan grinned. 'I admit, our numbers have been badly reduced by our recent activities and that after the final drop tomorrow night we won't be receiving any new men – so, yes, you're right, we need you to make up for our losses.' He spread his hands in a gesture of helplessness. 'But why not? What's good for us is good for you. Combined, we'll be twice as good as we are now, so it's well worth doing.'

'And where do you suggest we move to?' Lazenby asked.

'Even further south,' Callaghan replied. 'To the southernmost tip of the forest, well away from those Germans advancing from the north. Down near Aignay-le-Duc.'

'An area you know well,' Lazenby said.

'All to the good, Will.'

'And precisely where André Flaubert's Maquis are located.'

'That won't hurt us either. You never know when we'll need them.'

Lazenby glanced at Crittenden, who stared back thoughtfully, then gave him a nod. Turning back to Callaghan and Greaves, Lazenby raised his glass in another toast. 'All right, gentlemen, it's a deal. Let's drink to it.'

They touched glasses, toasting their forthcoming, unpredictable liaison.

'Who dares wins,' Captain Greaves said.

12

The move to Aignay-le-Duc was made two days later, D and C Squadrons travelling separately under cover of darkness. Like the previous hide of D Squadron, the new base was located in dense undergrowth, with the bell tents in a clearing hidden under a natural arch of trees and the lean-tos practically woven into the foliage to make them invisible from the air and difficult to see even at close quarters. Callaghan was thrilled by the new hide, though he expressed his concern that the absence of good paths might cause the new jeep tracks to be noticed.

'We have an effective but extraordinarily tedious way of preventing that,' Captain Lazenby replied.

'Oh?' Callaghan asked. 'What's that?'

'When a jeep is either leaving or returning to the camp, its two gunners have to walk for about half a mile behind it, covering the tyre tracks with vegetation. That means the jeeps arrive and depart very slowly, but at least it works.'

'My gunners will go mad when I tell them that,' Callaghan replied.

'They're probably mad already.'

Once the new hide had been completed, Callaghan sent a coded message on the radio, asking for a resup at 2200 hours that evening and giving details of the chosen DZ. As this drop was to include the last of his personnel replacements, a mere six men, he asked Lazenby to take him on a visit to the Maquis camp, which was in another part of the forest, about five miles away.

'Even our combined numbers are dangerously low,' Callaghan explained, 'so we might have to call on the Maquis, whether or not we like it. So let's all be sociable.'

Callaghan and Greaves drove with Lazenby, cruising in broad daylight through a landscape seemingly untouched by war and devoid of soldiers, friendly or otherwise. The day was bright and cold, and an autumn breeze was blowing. The softly rolling fields, as yet unharvested, and broken up by darker green hedgerows, forest and the occasional glittering stream, reminded all three officers of rural England, particularly Gloucestershire, where the regiment was presently based. Nevertheless, though no other soul or vehicles could be seen, all three officers had 9mm Sten guns resting across their laps, ready for use.

In the event, nothing happened and since the journey was so short and they were cruising at an average speed of forty miles per hour, they arrived at the Maquis camp in about ten minutes. Like the SAS camp, it was secreted in a clearing deep in the forest and had its tents and lean-tos carefully camouflaged with foliage. What surprised Callaghan and Greaves most, however, was the size of the supply dump they could see at the far edge of the clearing and the ammunition dump not far from it. They were even more surprised to see sandbagged gun emplacements bristling with Bofors anti-aircraft guns and even six-pounders. The Maquis had not had all that equipment when they split from the SAS two and a half weeks ago. In fact, they had had practically nothing.

After climbing out of the jeep, the three SAS officers were escorted by a man wearing a plain grey suit and a black beret, and carrying an American M1 carbine, to the largest tent in the camp. Inside, they found André seated in a canvas-covered folding chair with maps spread out on the trestle-table in front of him. Maxine was behind him, wearing an old British Army tunic with black sweater and trousers. A black beret perched jauntily on her thick, black hair, above her ivory-coloured face, made her look even more beautiful than normal. An M1 carbine was slung across her back and bandoliers of ammunition criss-crossed her slim, curvaceous body. When she looked up, she recognized the Englishmen, but did not smile at them. André, by contrast, grinned broadly and raised his right hand in greeting.

'Ah! My old friends, Captains Callaghan and Greaves! It is good to see you again. Please, be seated,' he said in English.

The three officers took chairs on the other side of the table, all aware that André was enjoying his role as commander and host. Before anyone could speak, he clapped his hands and asked Maxine to fetch the bottle of vermouth and five glasses. When she did so, taking them from a small cupboard on the floor of the tent, André poured everyone drinks and passed the glasses around.

'To General de Gaulle!' he said, holding up his glass. 'To the liberation of Paris!'

'To the King,' Callaghan rejoindered sardonically. They all drank, then Callaghan said in French: 'We wondered what had happened to you, André. We were a bit concerned.'

The Maquis leader just shrugged. 'Why should you be concerned? You asked us to go out on raids against the Germans and that's what we did. It is what we have *always* done.'

'But you didn't keep in touch,' Greaves said.

André shrugged again. 'I didn't think, Captain. We were too busy doing what we do best. What would we call you for?'

'We were supposed to be having a loose liaison.'

'That term means nothing to me. I only know that we have our own ways of doing things and that unfortunately you do not always approve of them. We like to do things as we have always done them and I decided that we do not need the assistance of the British Army – not even the SAS.'

'So why have you come here?' Maxine asked.

'For a pleasant reunion,' Callaghan replied without pause, 'and to find out just what you've been doing.'

'We have been doing what *you've* been doing,' Maxine replied without a smile. 'Blowing up bridges, railway lines and communications cables, stealing weapons and supplies, and, of course, killing Germans.'

'Yes,' Callaghan said. 'You're very good at that.'

'Count yourselves lucky that we are,' Maxine replied, her lovely brown eyes flashing a challenge.

'I noticed a lot of supplies and weapons outside. You didn't have those when you left us. Where did you get them?'

'From German convoys and trains. We don't attack and flee back into the woods as you do. When we attack, we finish what we start, killing all the German guards and taking their weapons and the supplies. So we kill for a purpose.'

Callaghan smiled. 'You're obviously well organized.'

André nodded. 'We are. Now we even operate our own stretch of railway line through this territory. It runs between two local stations taken over by us when we got rid of the Germans who were there. That railway line is invaluable, enabling us to bring in the kind of big guns we could not have had otherwise.'

'Yes,' Captain Lazenby said, 'we noticed when we came in. The Bofors and the six-pounders. They were taken off the Germans?'

'From German trains, yes. Probably stolen from the British.'

'No doubt,' Greaves said.

'So what have you *really* come here for?' the relentless Maxine asked.

'Because of our depleted strength,' Callaghan replied candidly, 'we've joined our forces with Captain Lazenby's D Squadron. Because the Germans were beating the forest north of his hide and would eventually have found it, we decided to move as far south as possible – to Aignay-le-Duc, which is where we are camped now.'

'This is our territory, Captain.'

'We can't go elsewhere and must remain here at least until General Patton's 3rd Army reaches Dijon.'

'As you are here to help liberate us, Captain, I can hardly tell you to leave,' André said generously. 'Besides, apart from not wishing to work your way, we are grateful for what you have done in France. Therefore, if there is any way we can help . . .'

That was precisely what Callaghan wanted to hear. 'We appreciate that you find it difficult to take orders from us,' he said, 'but have come here to ask you to keep the loose liaison open should we need to work, if not exactly together, then relatively closely, in the near future.'

'Agreed.'

'We would also appreciate it if you would include us in any local intelligence that you feel may be of benefit to us.'

'Agreed.'

Callaghan finished off his drink and placed his glass on the table. The others did the same, then Callaghan smiled, stood up and reached across the table to shake the Frenchman's hand. Thank you, André.'

'My pleasure,' André said in English.

Maxine just nodded solemnly as the three SAS officers stood up, left the tent, clambered into their jeep and headed back the way they had come, all aware that they would not get any sleep that day because they had to prepare for the resup drop that night.

The drop took place as scheduled in a field approximately 800 yards long and about three miles from the hide. As usual, a heavily armed SAS guard surrounded the field, facing out towards any possible advancing enemy forces. And as before, two more groups of SAS troopers were spaced well apart in lines that faced each other across the long leg of the L-shaped DZ, which was illuminated with three red lights and one white. Greaves stood at the end of the short leg of the L, flashing clearance to land with his Morse lamp while Corporal Jim Almonds used his S-phone as a homing beacon and for direct communication with the incoming aircraft's pilot.

The night was particularly dark, with heavy clouds obscuring the moon and stars, and an unseasonably fierce wind was blowing. The aircraft being used this time was a Douglas C-47 Dakota, powered by two Pratt & Whitney R-1830 1200-hp engines. Shortly after it had banked and made its first low-altitude run over the DZ, four white parachutes billowed out over each of the many crates it had dropped. The crates floated down and thudded into the soft, grassy earth even as the Dakota was disappearing in the dark sky to circle around and come back for its second run.

Knowing that the second drop would be the descent of the six SAS paratroopers, the men on the ground were particularly quick to run into the middle of the DZ to remove the crates and canisters, then clear the parachutes and other debris, including wood from smashed crates, from the area. They were already heaving the crates and canisters, all unopened since there were no jeeps, up into the Bedford QL trucks as the Dakota returned and the white parachutes of the paratroopers blossomed high in the ink-black sky.

The many men humping the crates and canisters into the trucks had been replaced at the DZ by a smaller group of men whose function was simply to welcome the six new arrivals, help them out of their parachute harnesses and then guide them to the jeeps that would take them back to the hide. Those men, expecting to see six parachutes billowing out high above them, were therefore shocked to see only five. Not knowing what was happening, they waited tensely on both sides of the DZ, watching the white parachutes float down out of a sky so dark that they couldn't even see the paratroopers.

Even as they were looking up, they all heard a thud on the ground just outside the DZ. Assuming that one of the paratrooper's leg bags had broken loose and crashed to earth, the watching men were not too concerned, remaining where they were until the 'chutes had collapsed to the ground and started whipping like great flags as the rolling paratroopers tried to tug the cords tight. Instantly, the welcoming teams rushed into the DZ to help the new arrivals.

'Shit!' the first paratrooper freed said in an anguished whisper. 'Oh, shit!'

'What?' Jacko asked, being the first out on the field. 'You're down, mate! Safe and sound! In one piece! Welcome to France!'

'Miller went down!' the man said in a choked voice, his breathing heavy and tortured. 'I'm convinced he went down, he was right in front of me, but when I went out I couldn't see his 'chute. I don't think it opened. Oh, shit, where *is* he?'

'Don't worry, we'll find him,' Jacko said, thinking: Only five parachutes. Five out of six. 'Now get out of your harness.' As the man was struggling to do so, being tugged sideways by the wind-whipped parachute on the end of his cords, Jacko turned to the rest of the welcoming party and bawled: 'Miller! Where's Miller? *Look for Miller*!'

Galvanized into action by the anxiety in Jacko's voice, the men, including the newly arrived paratroopers, started calling out the missing man's name and scattered across the DZ to find him. When, after about ten minutes, they had failed either to elicit a response from Miller or to find him in person, they made their way back to the trucks. However, just as they were climbing up into them, Rich's voice called out of the far side of the DZ: 'Over here!'

Immediately, the men, including the new arrivals, rushed back across the field to where they could see Rich frantically waving. When they reached him, they found Lance-Corporal Ron Miller at his feet, smashed into the soft earth and looking like a crimson jelly. There was no opened parachute near him.

'I've examined him,' Rich said, sounding shaky. 'Poor sod didn't have a prayer. One end of his static line looks singed and tattered. My guess is that acid somehow ate through it in the Dakota and his 'chute didn't even pull out of its pack. In other words, because some penguin back in England was careless in packing the poor bugger's 'chute, he went out of that Dakota without it. It's still right there in his backpack, tucked up nice and neat. Christ, don't even *talk* to me!'

As the Welshman turned away from the mangled corpse, the other men muttered various curses against the lazy bastard back in England whose carelessness had cost Miller his life.

Jacko brutally brought them back to reality by bawling: 'Don't just fucking stand there! Go and fetch a stretcher and get this body out of here. We haven't got all night!' Shocked back to their senses, four of the men raced off for a stretcher, always carried in one of the Bedfords for a tragic event such as this, while the others removed their small spades from their webbing and proceeded to scoop the soft soil out from under the dead paratrooper.

'Don't talk to me!' Rich repeated in a tone of voice that did not remotely resemble his own. 'Those lazy, murderous bastards!'

Jacko walked up to the Welshman and placed his hand on his broad shoulder, to gently, sympathetically, shake him.

'Yeah,' Jacko said. 'Right. But forget it, Rich. Fuck it. It's just one of them things.'

'Fucking penguins!' Rich exploded, venting his rage at those who packed the parachutes back in England and often did it carelessly, either out of exhaustion or, as the SAS would have it, out of pure laziness or indifference. 'Fuck 'em all!'

'Know just what you mean, mate,' said Jacko as comfortingly as he could.

A few minutes later, the four men who had run off returned with a stretcher, picked the bloody, sagging body of Lance-Corporal Miller up out of the hole created by his fall and the subsequent digging of the SAS troopers, rolled it on to the stretcher, then humped it back across the dark field to the waiting Bedford. Within minutes, the crater had been filled in by the other men and covered with loose foliage to render it invisible to prying eyes. Shortly after that, the trucks and jeeps moved out in single file, away from the DZ, heading back to the hide in the forest.

Lance-Corporal Miller, who had never fought his war, was buried with full military honours in the tiny churchyard of Aignay-le-Duc the following day.

13

Six hours after the ill-fated paratrooper had been buried, and two hours after last light, the combined C and D Squadrons commenced serious operations against the enemy, with separate patrols going out on all the main roads through the Forest of Châtillon. Determined this time to be as aggressive as possible, the group led by Captain Greaves, but with Sergeant Lorrimer's jeep out on point, parked, spaced well apart, on both sides of a road marked on their maps as a major MSR and waited patiently in the darkness to ambush the first German convoys that came along.

They did not have a long wait. The first German vehicles to pass, only thirty minutes later, were three canvas-topped supply trucks travelling at no more than thirty miles per hour with dimmed headlights. Greaves waited until the German column had drawn parallel to his own hidden line of parked vehicles, then gave the signal to open fire.

The savage roar of the combined twin Vickers was followed instantly by the smashing of the glass in the German trucks' windscreens and the demented whine of ricocheting .303-inch bullets. The first truck immediately careered off the road with a screeching of brakes and plunged nose first into the ditch at the far side. The middle car, which must have been loaded with ammunition, exploded with a deafening roar and became a ball of fire shuddering to a halt, into which the third truck then crashed.

As the dreadful screaming of the men in the cabin of the blazing truck rose briefly even above the harsh chatter of the Vickers, the flames from the burning vehicle, which were extraordinarily violent and of a dazzling whiteness, swept back to engulf the cabin of the truck that had smashed into it, producing more dreadful cries from the men trapped there. The SAS men not manning the machine-guns emptied their 9mm Sten guns and tommy-guns into the drivers' cabins to put them out of their misery, and as the men stopped screaming the canvas top of the third truck burst into flames. Within seconds, this fresh blaze had ignited the ammunition in that truck and it, too, exploded with a mighty roar, turning into a ball of white fire and billowing black smoke.

'Move out!' Greaves bawled into his S-phone.

Before any Germans who might have been following the first three trucks could pursue them, the SAS jeeps reversed on screeching tyres, then headed back into the forest by the same narrow track that had taken them to the MSR. Half an hour later they were again parked by the side of the MSR, but now ten miles east of their previous location, waiting for another convoy to pass. This time their victims were a convoy of ten German motor-cycle troops, all on powerful bikes, wearing heavy leather coats and steel helmets, with semi-automatic rifles slung across their backs. When the Vickers roared into action, the motor-cyclists were briefly caught in a dazzling web of phosphorescent green, blue and crimson lines created by the hail of mixed incendiary, tracer and armour-piercing bullets, which gave them no time to escape.

Chopped to pieces even before the other SAS troops had opened fire with their personal weapons, the Germans either fell off their wildly careering motor-cycles or were incinerated when their petrol tanks were pierced and exploded into flames. Within seconds, a nightmarish spectacle had unfolded, accompanied by deafening explosions and demented screams.

'Move out!' Greaves bawled into his S-phone.

Again the SAS jeeps reversed hurriedly, turned around and roared back the way they had come. Their third stop, forty minutes later, just before midnight, was ten miles further along the MSR, where it ran between the old market town of Auxerre on the River Yonne and Avallon, further south. Knowing that the Germans were beginning to evacuate the captured towns and villages of this area as Allied forces swept south from liberated Paris and Patton's 3rd Army closed in on Dijon from the east, Callaghan was confident that sooner or later more German columns would come along the MSR, fleeing from Auxerre.

This turned out to be true, though they had to wait in the darkness for nearly two hours. Meanwhile the moonlit sky directly above them filled up with an awesome number of Allied aircraft – Fortresses and Liberators of the US 8th and 9th Air Forces; RAF Handley-Page Halifaxes and Lancasters of RAF Bomber Command; and a protective umbrella of US Thunderbolts and RAF Spitfire fighters – all heading south-east. Minutes later, the muffled thunder of distant bombing could be heard and the dark sky beyond Dijon was fitfully illuminated by fans of silvery-white light where the bombs were exploding.

That's the area between Dijon and Belfort,' Greaves told Lorrimer through the S-phone. 'Patton must be preparing to make his final push to Dijon.'

'Which means Jerry will soon be swarming all over this place,' Lorrimer replied.

'Let's hope so, Sarge.'

Eventually, about two in the morning, as the immense Allied fleet of aircraft passed overhead and the distant muffled pounding continued, Greaves's expectations were fulfilled when an unusually large German convoy of what looked like troop trucks with dipped headlights came along the road from the direction of Auxerre, heading south to avoid Dijon. Realizing that he could well have a major fire-fight on his hands, but that the proximity of the German convoy made it too late to contact the other SAS men and tell them to make a tactical withdrawal, Greaves again waited until the passing convoy was parallel with his own hidden jeeps before slapping Jacko on the shoulder and bawling: 'Open fire!'

The combined roaring of Jacko and Rich's twin Vickers was the signal for the machine-gunners in the other SAS jeeps to open fire too, covering the passing convoy in the customary web of phosphorescent green, blue and crimson lines. The bedlam of the machine-guns was followed instantly by the shattering of windscreens, the popping of exploding tyres, the screeching of skidding tyres and brakes, then frantic bawling in German and the screams of wounded men. A couple of the trucks careered sideways and ploughed nose first into the ditch; two or three more crashed into each other as some braked unexpectedly; and the petrol tank of one of them was peppered with .303-inch bullets and exploded, engulfing the driver's cabin in a sheet of searing white flame that set fire to the men inside, who filled the air with their fearsome screams.

As German troops jumped out of the rear of the stalled trucks, unslinging their weapons even as their boots hit the ground, the SAS men not manning the machine-guns opened fire with Sten guns, tommy-guns and .303 Lee-Enfields, increasing the already deafening roar and cutting many of the Germans down before they could work out exactly where the fire was coming from.

Hearing the roar of a fighter plane and the chatter of its guns directly above him, even in the bedlam of the SAS attack, Greaves glanced up and saw a lone USAF Thunderbolt swooping down over the German column. The fighter's guns stitched parallel lines of spitting dust and gravel along the road, running right up to the first of the stalled German trucks, then tore through the trucks with a murderous fusillade that chopped the canvas covers to shreds and exposed the men screaming and dying inside.

As more of the Germans frantically tried to escape from the trucks, the Thunderbolt swept up and away to circle round before coming back for a second dive. Meanwhile, the SAS men continued the American's deadly handiwork by chopping down more of the Germans with their personal weapons while the twin Vickers continued to rake the trucks, peppering more petrol tanks and causing more deafening explosions of dazzling white flame and billowing black smoke.

Less than two minutes later the Thunderbolt swooped back down over the column with all its guns chattering noisily, again strafing the stalled, besieged convoy mercilessly. This time, however, the Germans returned the fire with a hail of bullets from an uncovered anti-aircraft gun and when the Thunderbolt had made its devastating run over the column and was ascending again, it was hit and left a trail of smoke behind it. High in the sky, it went into a spin and managed to level out long enough for the pilot to bale out. As his white parachute billowed like a flower in the dark sky, the Thunderbolt went out of control, going first into a spin, then into a nose dive, leaving a wavering smoke signature behind it as it plunged into the ground far away and exploded in a fan of silvery light. The parachute continued to drift gently to earth and had soon disappeared beyond a dark line of silhouetted trees to the east of Auxerre.

'Pull out!' Greaves bawled into his S-phone.

With the German trucks either destroyed completely or damaged beyond repair, and the enemy troops severely depleted, Greaves could see little point in remaining by the side of the road long enough to let the dazed survivors of the raid get their senses back and launch a counter-attack. Instead, as before, the SAS jeeps screeched into reverse, then turned away and raced back into the forest, using a secondary road that led them in a wide arc around Auxerre and on to Châtillon, some forty miles north of Dijon.

They had been driving for about half an hour when Jacko, who insisted on standing behind his twin Vickers in the lead jeep, driven by Sergeant Lorrimer, said: 'There's someone on the road straight ahead and he's waving at us, obviously wanting us to stop.'

'Is he armed?' Lorrimer asked, not sharing Jacko's more expansive view out of the jeep and straining to see through the darkness.

'No,' Jacko replied, though he cocked the Vickers all the same, 'but he might have armed friends in the trees at either side of the road. He's still frantically waving, though.' However, as the jeep drew closer to that dark figure on the road, Jacko spotted the flying jacket the man was wearing.

'Unless he's wearing stolen clothes, I think he's an American pilot,' he said.

'That would make sense,' Lorrimer replied. 'The pilot of that Thunderbolt came down in this general vicinity. We'll slow down until we can check, but keep your fingers on the triggers of those K guns and your eyes peeled for any movement on either side of the road.'

'Right, boss, will do.'

'Slowing down to check identity of possible downed US pilot,' Lorrimer told Greaves, in the jeep behind him, on his S-phone. 'If he checks out, we'll pick him up.'

'Confirmed,' Greaves replied. 'Over and out.'

Lorrimer slowed down and eventually stopped right in front of the man in the road. The other jeeps came to a stop behind him and the machine-gunners each covered his own side of the tree-lined road. The man was stocky and brown-haired, and his flying jacket, Lorrimer noticed, was slightly singed, though he was grinning broadly as he held his hands in the air.

'Don't shoot!' he shouted melodramatically. 'Cap'n Oliver Ladd of the US 8th Air Force. You guys shot up that German convoy back near Auxerre?'

'Correct,' Lorrimer said.

The pilot lowered his hands to spread them in the air, palms up, his grin still wide. 'Well, I was flying the Thunderbolt that shot that convoy up, helping you guys out. You might've seen me bale out.'

'We did,' Lorrimer said, jerking his left thumb to indicate that the American should take the seat beside him. 'Hop in, Captain.'

'Call me "Olly",' said the pilot, positively beaming as he climbed in beside Sergeant Lorrimer, waved to Jacko and Rich, and then at the jeeps lined up behind them, before settling into his seat. Starting up the jeep and moving forward again, Sergeant Lorrimer introduced Captain Ladd to Jacko and Rich, then said: 'So where did you land, Olly?'

Ladd waved his right hand to indicate the field they were just leaving behind them. 'Over in that cow pasture,' he said with a lazy drawl. 'Ankle-deep in mud, but otherwise OK. I buried the 'chute over there.'

'What's the accent?'

'Fort Worth, Texas. A Texan born and bred.'

Using the S-phone, Lorrimer called back to Greaves and gave him Ladd's details, then clipped the phone back to his chest webbing and asked: 'You were part of that fleet of aircraft heading beyond Dijon?'

'Right,' Ladd replied. 'We were going to bomb and strafe the hell out of the area between there and Belfort.'

'In support of General Patton's 3rd Army?'

'You got it, friend.'

'Does that mean the final push on Dijon has begun?'

'Correct. It's all over but for the singing, Sarge. At least in this area. You guys have done a really fine job of keeping Jerry distracted.'

'And we're not finished yet,' Lorrimer told him.

'You mind if I stick with you guys for a while?'

'I don't think you've much choice.'

'You SAS?'

'That's right, Captain.'

'We've heard an awful lot about you guys and all of it good.'

'That's nice,' Lorrimer said.

'So where are you going next?' the American asked.

Lorrimer shrugged. 'We don't know. We just drive around until we find something. Tonight we've been hitting the MSR at ten or fifteen-mile intervals. We did a fair bit of damage.'

'Well, I don't know if this is of interest or not, but when I parachuted into that field, I nearly fell on the Frog farmer who owns it. When I asked him if the area was safe, he told me no, that there was a German headquarters in a farm near Châtillon. An enthusiastic old buzzard, well down on the Krauts and well up on weaponry, he told me he thought that it might be a good target for some men with mortars or big guns. I notice you've got mortars back there, so it might be worth checking out.'

'Indeed it might,' Lorrimer replied. Unclipping the S-phone, he called back to Greaves and passed on Ladd's information. Greaves agreed that nothing would be lost in reconnoitring the area, so they changed direction accordingly and headed for Châtillon. It was just before dawn when, at a roadside farmhouse not far from the town, they stopped to seek further information.

Covered by the Vickers of Jacko and Rich, as well as those in the second jeep, but with Lorrimer's Sten gun at the ready just in case, the sergeant and Greaves walked up the path to the farmhouse, carefully looked in through both front windows, one man at each, and saw the farmer and his wife, the latter still in her nightdress, sitting at the kitchen table, eating a breakfast of fried eggs and crusty rolls.

The two SAS men converged on the front door, which Lorrimer hammered on with his clenched fist. When the farmer's flushed, well-fed face appeared at the left-hand window, his gaze sleepily curious at this early hour, Greaves stepped away from the door to let himself be seen. Eventually, satisfied that they were British, the farmer opened the door, greeted them in French, then switched to passable English for the rest of the conversation.

'Yes, Captain,' he said, automatically addressing the man with senior rank. 'What can I do for you?'

'Do you know of a nearby farm being used as a German headquarters?'

The farmer nodded. 'I believe one is being so used, but unfortunately I do not know which one.' He smiled and scratched his pink, blue-veined nose. 'But maybe I can find out for you. Step inside, *messieurs*.'

Captain Greaves and Lorrimer followed the farmer into what appeared to be his living-room. It contained mildewed sofas and soft chairs, a tremendous amount of clutter, and a row of recently killed rabbits, strung up by their hind feet on a string that ran above the fireplace. Greaves shivered, but Lorrimer just grinned.

'I will ring the Mayor,' the farmer told them, as if it was a perfectly normal thing to do at that time of the morning. 'If anyone knows where the Germans are staying, he'll be the one. As the Mayor he has to liaise with them, so surely he'll know.'

He dialled a number, waited for what seemed like a long time, then bid someone good morning, possibly the Mayor's wife or child, and asked for the Mayor. After another lengthy pause, the farmer bid the dignitary good morning, explained that he had some British soldiers in his farmhouse and added that they wanted to know which local farm the Germans were presently using as their headquarters. He listened carefully, then thanked the Mayor for his information and. put the phone down.

'He was most obliging, since he is grateful to the British,' he said. 'Unfortunately, he told me that the farm recently used as a German headquarters has since been evacuated. He also told me to inform you that because of the last Allied bombing raid and the imminent advance of General Patton, the main garrison of Châtillon is being relieved by Panzer

Grenadiers from Montbard. He would not be averse to the idea of your men attacking them and getting rid of them for good.'

'How many are there?' Greaves asked, hardly able to believe he was receiving valuable local intelligence in this casual manner, but noticing the amused grin on Lorrimer's face.

'Approximately 150 Germans with twenty trucks in the precincts of the château. However, more are expected tomorrow. Perhaps you could wait for them.'

'Perhaps we could,' Greaves said. 'What's the most convenient way into the town?'

'Turn left at my front gate, then follow the road around to the aerodrome. There are no planes there, so it is rarely guarded and will give you easy access to the town. All of the Germans, I believe, are in the château, so you should get there unmolested.'

'Thank you, *monsieur*. You've been very helpful.'

After returning to his jeep, Greaves directed the column to the aerodrome, which they reached in less than ten minutes. As the farmer had stated, the aerodrome was completely deserted and they were able to drive across the airstrip and enter the town by a side road. The first people to see them, some farmworkers, men and women, looked up in surprise as they drove past.

Continuing through the town, they emerged at the other side without encountering a single German and found themselves at a dried-up river bed, which was marked on their map and ran to the foot of the hill on which the château stood. When they reached the hill, Greaves ordered the column to stop and wait for him, then turned to Lorrimer and simply said: 'Bring a rope.' When Lorrimer had obligingly slung a knotted abseiling rope with a steel grappling hook at the end over his right shoulder, he and Greaves clambered up the steep slope until they came to the rear wall of the château.

Lorrimer unwound the rope and threw it up the side of the thirty-foot-high wall, until the hook had caught on the sharp-edged brick. After checking that it would hold by tugging vigorously and repeatedly at it, he placed his feet on the lower brickwork, leant well back and began expertly to scale the sheer wall, reaching the top in no time at all. He then threw the end of the knotted rope back down and Greaves made the same arduous, dangerous climb.

During their ascent the two men were watched by many amazed townspeople, from the upper windows of the tall houses surrounding the château. Once on top of the wall, precariously balanced on the narrow ledge that ran around it, they were able to look down into the courtyard and take note of the number of men and vehicles there, as well as the nature of the heavy weapons spread out around them. But not for very long, for within seconds, they had been spotted by some of the German soldiers in the courtyard and warning shouts were followed almost instantly by a fusillade of rifle fire that sent bullets ricocheting noisily about them, chipping off splinters of stone and creating blinding clouds of dust that billowed up from around their feet.

'Let's get back down,' Greaves said.

'No argument, boss.'

One after the other, the two men abseiled back down the wall as bullets ricocheted off the inside ledge on which they had been standing moments before. Just as the second to descend, Sergeant Lorrimer, reached the ground, half a dozen helmeted German troops ran out of the opened back gate of the château, firing sub-machine-guns on the move. Instantly, the SAS men in the jeeps below the hill opened up with their Vickers, firing in an arc that kicked up the dirt all around the Germans and then made most of them convulse frantically amid clouds of dust in the seconds before they died. The few who survived were backing into the rear gateway, still firing on the move, as Lorrimer and Greaves ran back down the slope and climbed hurriedly into their respective jeeps. As the vehicles roared away from the hill, the Vickers in the last jeep, fired by Jacko and Rich, kept the Germans in the gateway pinned down to let the convoy race out of range.

'Gee, you guys are really something!' Olly Ladd exclaimed, grinning excitedly. 'I mean, scaling that goddam wall! I'd heard you guys were something special and now I believe it.'

'It's all in a day's work,' Lorrimer replied as he sped away from the château. 'And the day isn't over yet.'

Indeed, it wasn't. As they turned off along a track that led back into the forest, they saw a convoy of four trucks heading for Châtillon on a road running parallel to their own. Standing up to use a hand signal, Greaves, hoping to catch the Germans at the next junction, indicated that the jeeps should turn around and drive back the way they had come. Unfortunately, they were too late to intercept the Germans. The sudden, shocking sound of massed rifle fire indicated that the Germans had been stopped by André Flaubert and his fellow Maquisards further along the Châtillon road.

'Keep going!' Greaves ordered with another hand signal.

To the delight of Olly Ladd, the SAS jeeps continued to race along the narrow track until they were approaching the broader road used as an MSR. Before actually getting there, the jeeps slowed down and crept along in low gear, trying to make as little noise as possible. Given the bedlam being created by the combined fire of the Germans and the Maquis, this was not too difficult and soon the SAS were close enough to get a good view of the two warring sides.

The Maquisards had set up a roadblock of fallen trees and foliage. Now they were firing along the road at the Germans hiding behind their four blocked trucks, which they had parked across the road for their own protection. As the Germans had their backs to the SAS jeeps and could not hear their quiet approach because of the clamorous gunfire, the SAS men were able to drive to a distance within the firing range of their personal weapons and open up with those, as well as with the more powerful mounted Vickers.

Two of the trucks, their petrol tanks riddled by .303-inch bullets, exploded into flames, instantly killing some of the Germans kneeling behind them and setting two others on fire. As the burning Germans ran about yelling dementedly, only to be cut down by a merciful hail of SAS bullets, the combined might of the various SAS guns sent a murderous fusillade into the backs of the other Germans. Shocked, the few left turned around in a vain attempt to fire back. As they did so, the Maquisards used the respite to clamber over their makeshift barricade and advance along the road, firing on the move, thus catching the last of the Germans in a deadly cross-fire.

A few minutes later the SAS men and the Maquisards were standing over the dead bodies of the German troops sprawled bloodily across the road, behind and between their four trucks, two of which were still blazing and filling the air with boiling, black smoke. The battle was over.

Later that afternoon, after they had had a good sleep, every officer, NCO and other soldier in C and D Squadrons reunited at their hide in the forest near Aignay-le-Duc, drove to André Flaubert's camp five miles away and celebrated their joint victory with a typically lengthy French lunch of excellent local dishes, wine and calvados. Even the normally suspicious Maxine was in good spirits and looked lovelier than ever. In the course of the lunch, provided by the Maquis from their bountiful supply dump, the bearded, dirty men from both sides treated each other with respect and, under the influence of too much wine, repeatedly toasted one another and formed maudlin friendships that were unlikely to last much past dawn.

André, now looking more favourably upon the SAS, agreed with the officers, including D Squadron's Captain Lazenby, that the combined SAS and Maquis should attack Châtillon at dawn the next day, while the German relief was still going on. He also agreed to supply five hundred men if the SAS would give them enough petrol for their trucks. When Callaghan said that this would be arranged, the men drank another toast to victory and the party continued, not breaking up until last light when everyone was very drunk.

When they woke at first light to commence the raid that would finally chase the Germans out of the area and pave the way for the last push of General Patton's 3rd Army, nearly all the SAS men were suffering from excruciating hangovers. Nevertheless, they knew that this was to be a decisive battle.

14

It was just after dawn and the light was still pearly grey when the first group of SAS troops, commanded by Captain Greaves, crossed the deserted aerodrome and occupied the Montbard-Dijon crossroads. Once there, buffeted by a sharp wind and showered with stinging dust, they began setting up a defensive perimeter that included a 3-inch mortar and a Bren gun, both behind sandbagged gun emplacements, and a team of men armed with .303-inch Lee-Enfield bolt-action rifles, 9mm Sten guns and tommy-guns, lying in shallow scrapes at strategic points at the side of each of the four roads, all near the junction and each other.

'Where the hell are the Maquis?' Greaves asked anxiously, knowing that at that moment the rest of the SAS men were reliably taking up their own positions in Châtillon and around the château, but feeling nervous because the resistance fighters had not shown up at the RV near the SAS's forest hide.

'Probably still sleeping it off,' Captain Lazenby said sardonically, knowing the Maquis well. 'Either that or our proud little friend André, and his mistrustful Maxine, have changed their minds and decided to let us go it alone.'

'That would be a right bloody help,' Greaves muttered softly.

'Anyway, you'd best be on your way to set up that mortar.'

'Right,' Lazenby said.

Leaving Greaves and his men to complete their defensive perimeter around the junction, Lazenby and the other half of the group, consisting of a foot patrol following a jeep carrying a second mortar, went along the road to find a position that would allow the weapon to attack the north face of the château. Having found such a position on the wooded lower slopes south of the château, he called a halt and climbed down from the jeep, followed by his two-man mortar team. While the rest of the men prepared their personal weapons, the two in charge of the mortar dug a shallow scrape, placed the steel base plate in it, supported it with a couple of shells in tightly packed soil and gravel, then fixed the mortar to the base plate and piled a total of forty-eight bombs beside it, in readiness for action. The first shot fired by that weapon would be the signal for the others to begin the attack.

While Greaves's men were taking control of the junction and Lazenby was settling in with his mortar and assault teams south of the château, Callaghan was moving another forty men by jeep into the town, where, under the curious, hopeful gaze of the townspeople, most of whom were emerging silently from their homes to look on, they occupied all the main junctions leading into the market square.

'Where are the bloody Maquis?' Callaghan growled, glancing anxiously up and down the various streets running into the square and seeing only more curious inhabitants.

'Buggered if I know,' Lorrimer replied. 'Whether they turn up or not is anybody's guess.'

'I'll kill that bloody André if he doesn't show,' Callaghan said, displaying a flash of the anger for which he was well known and which had often got him into trouble in the past. 'With my bare hands!'

'I'd like to be here to see it,' Lorrimer replied, grinning, though secretly just as anxious, 'but I've got to go and cut those military telephone cables.'

'Yes, you do that, Sarge.'

Taking two of the jeeps and their three-man teams, with Jacko and Rich manning the twin Vickers guns in his own vehicle, Sergeant Lorrimer drove to the Troyes – Chaumont crossroads. There he asked for one man from each vehicle to climb the telegraph poles and cut the cables with their wire-cutters. One of the 'volunteers' was Jacko. As he and Corporal Reg Seekings from the second jeep were cutting the wires, the other two men, Rich and Corporal Benny Bennett, remained standing at the mounted guns in their respective jeeps, scanning the Troyes and Chaumont roads for signs of advancing enemy convoys.

There was no sign of the Germans.

The Maquis did not materialize either.

South of the château, Lazenby checked his wrist-watch and waited for the second hand to move to 0700 hours. He raised his right hand, concentrating on the hand creeping round the dial, and then, at exactly 0700 hours, dropped his hand to his side.

At this signal, the first mortar bomb was dropped into the tube and fired immediately. A muffled thump was followed by a cloud of smoke from the tube, then, mere seconds later, by a much louder explosion that brutally shattered the morning's silence as the bomb erupted near the top of the slope, just in front of the northern wall of the château, hurling up a spectacular storm of soil and gravel, but leaving the wall untouched.

The instant that single explosion was heard some of the SAS men from Callaghan's group in the square advanced up the road towards the front of the château, preparing to engage with the German troops they knew would come down eventually, either to attack or to escape. At that same moment Lorrimer's team were kicking the chopped military communications cables to the side of the roads at the Troyes – Chaumont crossroads. This done, they climbed back into their jeeps to take up positions behind the Vickers guns and, if necessary, either prevent the German soldiers in the town from escaping this way or stop reinforcements from entering the town in support of their comrades.

'Where the hell are those bloody Maquis?' Sergeant Lorrimer asked rhetorically as the second mortar bomb fired by Lazenby's team exploded on the northern slope of the château, followed almost immediately by a third and a fourth. By the time the third shell had exploded, the mortar team had ascertained the correct calibration and were pleased to see a great chunk of the wall spewing outwards in a billowing cloud of stones, dust and pulverized cement.

Other bombs lobbed off in quick succession completely devastated the northern wall, provoking a fusillade of small-arms fire from along its ramparts. Simultaneously, the front gates of the south side opened and a horde of steel-helmeted Panzer troops raced out and marched down the road to take command of the town, unaware that the SAS were already in position on both sides of the road leading into the market square.

When the enemy troops were within range, the SAS men opened fire with their combined .303-inch Lee-Enfields, 9mm Sten guns, tommy-guns and two bipod-mounted Bren guns. They were followed immediately by a succession of bombs from another 3-inch mortar.

Around and between the advancing Panzer troops the earth became a violent convulsion of erupting soil and gravel, flying stones, spitting, swirling dust and smoke as the exploding bombs and rain of bullets took their toll. Some of the Germans did, however, emerge from the hellish murk and noise to hurl 'potato-mashers'. Exploding at both sides of the road, the grenades tore three of the SAS men to shreds, seriously wounded another and left half a dozen more temporarily dazed. This was enough to enable the rest of the Panzer troops to rush down the hill, hurling more potato-mashers and firing their Schmeissers on the move, forcing the SAS to make a tactical retreat back towards the town.

Fifteen minutes into the battle, a column of about thirty German trucks containing the relief party arrived at the river bridge near Greaves's position on the Montbard-Dijon cross-roads. Though his jeep, manned by Harry-boy Turnball and Neil Moffatt, was in the middle of the road, Greaves let the Germans approach to within twenty yards before he gave the order to open fire.

The instant the twin Vickers roared into action, the 3-inch mortar and Bren gun in the sandbagged gun positions opened up as well, followed by the machine-guns of the other SAS jeeps and the personal weapons of the men in the shallow scrapes by the sides of the roads that converged at the junction.

This combined fire-power was devastating, tearing the first trucks in the German convoy to shreds, making the first two skid in opposite directions across the road, and then igniting the ammunition in the third, fourth and fifth. The subsequent explosions were awesome to behold, throwing up loose gravel, soil and debris in great mushrooms that sent back to earth a rain of blazing pieces of canvas, scorched, buckled metal, glistening shards of glass from the broken windscreens, scraps of uniform and dismembered limbs. The German troops who survived this and managed to spill out of the back of the remaining trucks were caught in a savage crossfire of mixed incendiary, tracer and armour-piercing bullets that resembled a brilliant pyrotechnic display. Amid that bizarrely beautiful spectacle the Germans shuddered, jerked spasmodically, twisted into grotesque shapes, screamed horribly, dropped to the ground and expired.

As most of their comrades were dying in the hail of bullets, a motor-cycle with a sidecar carrying an armed trooper broke away from the end of the convoy and raced off in a cloud of dust, travelling in a broad arc that brought it around to one of the roads leading to the Troyes – Chaumont crossroads. Before noticing the SAS men placed there, the motor-cyclist turned on to the road and headed straight for the bridge leading to the junction.

'Get those bastards!' Lorrimer bawled.

The combined Vickers of the two jeeps at the crossroads roared into action as the motor-cycle came up over the slight hump of the picturesque stone bridge that spanned the river running past the town. The startled motor-cyclist just had time to catch a glimpse of the SAS jeeps facing him before he was almost chopped in half by a fusillade from the two machine-guns and lost control of his machine. Even as the bike was careering towards the side of the bridge, the desperate passenger instinctively let off a short burst from a Schmeisser. Short it surely was – because at that precise moment another hail of .303-inch bullets turned the sidecar into a hell of flying wood chips and dust even as the machine flew off the side of the bridge, sailed through the air and then plunged into the river, the driver and passenger both flying out even further before also splashing into the water.

The steel helmet of the passenger bounced against the bank, then rolled down into the river. Water eddied around the wrecked motor-cycle as it sank out of sight.

The bodies of the motor-cyclist and his passenger sank briefly and then bobbed up again, letting the stunned SAS men see, as the latter turned in the swirling water, a skein of long, golden hair spreading out in the bloody water.

'Oh, shit!' Jacko exclaimed. 'It was a bleedin' woman.'

'Bleeding now all right,' said Rich, often soft-hearted yet just as often coldly pragmatic. 'Bleeding and dead.'

The sounds of battle reverberated through the streets of the town behind them – rattling Brens, roaring Vickers, whining and ricocheting bullets, the distant thump of mortars, followed by noisier explosions – making them all glance back in that direction.

'Sounds hot back there,' Lorrimer said.

It was. By this time, Captain Greaves, knowing that no more German reinforcements would be arriving, had led his men away from the appalling carnage at the Montbard-Dijon cross-roads and back into the town square to lend support to Callaghan's group. Once there, Greaves took a Bren for himself and, balancing it precariously on the nearest wall, 'hosepiped' the advancing Panzer troops with crimson tracer. As he was doing so, the gun jammed.

Cursing to himself, Greaves tried releasing the mechanism and, glancing up, saw Olly Ladd joyfully firing a 9mm Sten gun from the hip, raking it from left to right to give himself the widest possible arc of fire. Even as some of the advancing Panzer troops were cut down by the American's fire, a German bullet blew the top of his head off, making him drop the Sten gun and jerk violently sideways, almost backwards. Then he walked a few yards, like some ghastly apparition, his exposed brains lifted up on a rising tide of blood as his knees gradually gave way beneath him. Eventually, blood still spurting from his shattered head, he collapsed, slid down the wall of a house, fell sideways and rolled on to his back. A Frenchman took hold of the pilot's ankles and dragged him into the hallway of the house, no doubt thinking he was still alive and could be saved.

Greaves could hear shooting from the far side of the square, as well as firing from behind the château, so he knew that Callaghan and Lazenby were still engaged. Glancing across the square, he saw the rest of Callaghan's men firing on the move as they retreated back down the slope leading up to the front of the château. Other men were doing the same in the other streets leading back into the square.

Suddenly, to Greaves's surprise and amusement, after the brutality of Ladd's death, a pretty French girl with long, jet-black hair and wearing a vivid blue, figure-hugging, low-cut dress, leaned out the top window of her house and gave the V sign to the embattled SAS men. Some of the SAS men actually stopped firing long enough to wave back and either cheer or wolf-whistle. Then they went back to attacking the Germans.

Shaking his head in amusement, Greaves returned to the task of unjamming his Bren gun, managed to free it, then rested the barrel on the wall and began firing again at the four Germans he saw advancing down one of the side streets. All of them were bowled over like skittles, leaving the street clear for the moment.

Just then, Callaghan and his team came backwards into the square, crouched low and firing on the move. Greaves gave them cover by firing his Bren at the Panzer troops swarming down the slope from the château. He was aided in this by the

SAS troops grouped around him and soon Callaghan was right there beside him. Callaghan stopped firing his Sten gun, straightened up, removed his red beret from his head with a flourish and wiped sweat from his dust-smeared forehead.

'Those bloody Panzer boys don't give up easily,' he said. Placing his beret back on his head and carefully adjusting its position, he continued: 'Got to hand it to them: they're damn persistent. Still fighting their way down from the château. On the other hand, they're so confused about what's happening that they've started mortaring their own side. Any sign of the French?'

'No,' Greaves replied.

'Then I think we'd better get out of here and give ourselves time to reconsider the situation and, perhaps, find out just what happened to them.'

'I agree. Shall I give the signal to withdraw?'

'Please do.'

As Lazenby's mortar fired yet again from the wooded slopes on the northern side of the château, Greaves marched boldly into the middle of the square, waved to the girl in the upstairs window, then fired two Very lights into the air, signalling that the various SAS groups scattered around the town and the château should withdraw. Then, waving one last time to the French girl, he and the other men, including Callaghan and Lorrimer, piled back into their jeeps and raced out of town, back to the forest. There they hoped to tuck into a well-earned breakfast and, more importantly, receive an explanation regarding the missing Maquis.

15

They didn't make it as far as the hide – for breakfast or anything, else. As his own jeep had been knocked out during the battle in Châtillon, Captain Callaghan had decided to march back on foot with seven of his men. On his way back across the formerly deserted aerodrome, he met André and Maxine marching across the airstrip with nearly eighty of the promised five hundred Maquisards strung out in loose file formation behind them. Almost exploding, the volatile Callaghan hurried up to the Maquis leader and screamed: 'Where the hell were you?'

André gave his familiar carefree shrug. 'It was not my fault,' he explained. 'I was up an hour before dawn to go looking for the other Maquisards, who I thought were in a separate camp in the forest. But they had moved on without telling me . . .'

'Bloody typical!' Callaghan interjected.

'. . . and so I had to return to my own camp and prepare my own men.'

'This lot?' Callaghan said, waving his free hand to indicate the eighty-odd men and women pressing up behind André and Maxine.

'Yes. However, when I told them that the other four hundred would not be coming with us, they decided to have a meeting to see if they should still come. Naturally, this took time and . . .'

'They decided to have a bloody meeting?' Callaghan bawled. 'We're fighting a war here!'

'*We're* fighting a war!' Maxine exploded with a ferocity to match Callaghan's. 'And we're doing it our way.'

'And your way means promising to help us, only to leave us stranded?'

'We work by democratic rule. If anyone disagrees with a plan, it must be discussed.'

'And in this case,' André added, 'the loss of the other four hundred Maquisards made some of my men think this battle would lead to too many casualties.'

'So you left us to get on with it on our own!'

'No!' Maxine snapped. 'Even though we all agreed that the battle would be too costly, in the end we voted to come, not only because we had already committed ourselves to you, but also because we wanted to minimize your losses. You should be grateful, not angry, Captain.'

In fact, Callaghan was so angry that he had to turn away from them and take deep, even breaths to control himself. One of those who had decided to come with him on foot was Sergeant Bob Tappman and when Callaghan saw his sly grin, it helped him cool down and act more diplomatically.

'All right,' he said, turning back to André and Maxine, 'I'll accept that. I'm sorry I got a bit annoyed, but I'm sure you understand. We left a lot of dead SAS men back there and it still isn't finished.'

'I understand, Captain,' André said, then shrugged again. 'So let's finish it.'

'I'm worried about the Germans killing off any wounded SAS men that they find, so I want to go straight back. If I call Captain Greaves, already back at the hide, and ask him to return and give us support, will you undertake to help my small group mount another attack right now?'

'Yes.'

'Good.'

Callaghan immediately removed his lightweight S-phone from its aluminium box strapped to his chest webbing and used it to contact Greaves, who had just arrived back in the hide. When the situation was explained to Greaves, he agreed to forget breakfast and return immediately to the town with his men, hopefully to meet up with Callaghan's group in the market square. Satisfied, Callaghan replaced the S-phone, then, gripping his Sten gun in his right hand, waved the weapon above his head and bawled: 'Move out!'

With the eighty well-armed Maquisards behind them, the nine SAS men from the three destroyed jeeps marched resolutely back to the town, crossing the low, humpback bridge over the river and then entering a street that led them directly down to the market square. As the SAS men entered that street, the Maquis were splitting up into six separate groups and circling the small town to enable each group to tackle a separate street. Going down the street he had chosen, Callaghan ordered his men to press themselves against the walls of the houses, hug the doorways, and move as quickly and as quietly as possible from one doorway to the next, so minimizing the chance of being hit by German snipers.

In fact, they managed to get down nearly all the way to the market square without interference. When close enough to see the square itself, they noted that it was filled with Panzer troops who were clearly regrouping to defend those clambering into trucks, preparing to flee the town. There was also a German armoured car in the square.

During the previous engagement, Harry-boy Turnball had removed a bazooka from a dead SAS trooper. Now, using hand signals, Callaghan indicated that he should set it up, aim for the armoured car, and fire at Callaghan's order, which would also be the signal for the rest of the men to attack with personal weapons and hand-grenades. Harry-boy duly dropped to one knee, adjusted the bazooka on his right shoulder, let himself be steadied by his friend Neil Moffatt, then squinted along the sight. At another hand signal from Callaghan he fired the bazooka.

The backblast punched Harry-boy backwards and the flying shell left a smoke signature that ran straight from Harry-boy to the armoured car. The Panzer troops had heard the backblast and were starting to look around just as the shell made a direct hit and the armoured car blew up with a deafening roar, filling the air with debris and bowling over some of the Germans. Instantly, before the other Panzer troops had realized what was happening, the SAS men spreading along both sides of the street around Harry-boy opened fire with their Sten guns, tommy-guns and .303-inch Lee-Enfield bolt-action rifles, cutting down the Germans they could see framed by the walls at the end of the street. At practically the same time, the sound of firing came from the other streets where the Maquis were using the same tactics.

'They're scattering!' Callaghan bawled. 'Watch out for the corners!'

While the German troop trucks started rumbling out of the square into what they thought were safe streets, the Panzer troops attempted to give them cover by dividing into teams that took one corner each of a street. From there they attacked the

SAS or Maquis by leaning in and out to fire short bursts from their sub-machine-guns. Callaghan's group returned this fire by hugging the doorways and ducking in and out in a similar manner, also firing savage bursts that hit very few Panzer troops but at least ensured that they could not move up the street.

After ten minutes of this, just as Callaghan was wondering how to break the deadlock and get his men on the move, Lorrimer's jeep came racing down the narrow street with Jacko and Rich already firing their deadly twin Vickers at opposite corners. Their sustained fire was enough to devastate the corner walls, fill the air with flying cement and dust, and keep the Germans on both sides pinned down until the jeep was racing out past the street corners and into the square. As it did so, the two gunners swung their weapons in tight arcs and kept firing, massacring the Germans huddled behind the walls.

Cheering, Callaghan's men leapt out from the doorways and raced down behind the jeep towards the square. As they emerged from the street, they saw other SAS jeeps racing into the square from the other side-streets, with the gunners firing their Vickers at the Germans huddling at the corners. Those jeeps were followed by hordes of Maquisards, who were cheering and firing their weapons at the same time.

Racing at the crouch across the square towards where Greaves's jeep was screeching to a halt, Callaghan heard explosions from different directions just outside the town. Glancing back over his shoulder as he ran, he saw ugly clouds of smoke billowing up beyond the surrounding houses, from what appeared to be the vicinity of the outlying crossroads. Callaghan then reached Greaves's jeep and dropped down beside him.

'I posted jeep ambushes on all the main roads leading out of the town,' Greaves explained, 'to stop the German trucks from leaving. Sounds like they succeeded.'

Callaghan glanced over the roofs and saw the columns of smoke on all sides – clearly the product of bazookas and Lewes bombs. 'I think you're right,' he told Greaves. No sooner had he spoken than the sound of Sten guns, tommy-guns and Lee-Enfield rifles came from the nearby streets. 'The Germans who escaped from the trucks must be retreating back into the town, pursued by our men,' he said. 'In some of the streets they'll be trapped between the men pursuing them and the Maquis or SAS troops down here. But some of the streets are unprotected, as are the narrow lanes connecting them, so I think we'll have to get the men to spread out and clear the whole town in a close-combat mop-up.'

'I don't think you have to tell them that,' Greaves replied, leaning sideways and peering around the front of the jeep. 'They seem to be doing that already.'

Callaghan saw immediately that this was true. With most of the Germans already cleared from the market square, even the SAS gunners manning the mounted Vickers were jumping down off the jeeps, carrying their personal weapons at the ready, and chasing the rest of the Germans into the streets leading out of the square. Once in that maze of narrow streets and criss-crossing lanes, close combat between small groups or individuals became unavoidable.

Jacko, Rich, Harry-boy and Neil were operating as an extremely efficient four-man team, each protecting the other as they clambered over the low walls dividing the backyards of houses, taking pot-shots at the Germans trying to escape by doing likewise.

The Germans were being trapped in a pincer movement, with the SAS and the Maquis closing in on all sides. Jacko knew just how frightened they must be, and why they could not afford to surrender, when, from his vantage-point on top of a wall, he saw three of them trapped in a pretty, tree-lined cul-de-sac. Backed up against a white-painted wall by a group of resistance fighters, including the sharpshooting Maxine, the Panzer troops had no choice but to drop their weapons and surrender. In fact, one of them had scarcely managed to get his hands above his head before he was chopped down by a combined blast from two Maquis carbines. Even as he convulsed, was slammed back into the wall, then slid down it like a punctured balloon, his two companions were turning away to face the wall with their hands high. Without hesitation, Maxine stepped up to them, raised what looked like a Luger in her right hand, and blew the back of both men's heads off. She and her fellow Maquisards were already running back out of the cul-de-sac to find more Germans as the last two were collapsing, leaving a trail of bright-red blood on the pretty white wall.

Instinctively understanding that Maquis justice had been bred from years of torment and torture of the French by the Germans, Jacko ignored what he had seen and clambered over another wall, following Rich, Harry-boy and Neil. After climbing over the last wall in the row of back gardens, he dropped down beside his mates, glanced left and right along the narrow, winding lane, then followed them along it until reaching another street. Leading out of town and into the square, it had fights going on at both ends, with a mixture of SAS and Maquisards showing no mercy to the Germans trying to battle their way out in one of two directions.

Out of range of both groups of Germans, Jacko and the others raced across the street, explored another narrow, dark lane and emerged on to the parallel street just as a group of about thirty German troops, all on bicycles, were coming up the hill in the hope of getting out of town. Instantly, the SAS men dropped back into the shelter of the narrow lane, but only three of them made it before the first of the Germans had let their bicycles fall to the ground, swung their Schmeissers up and fired a frantic burst.

Jacko was piling into Rick and Neil behind the shelter of the wall when he heard a truly dreadful sound from just behind him. Disentangling himself from his two mates, who were already swinging their weapons up to fire, he glanced back and saw Harry-boy writhing on the ground, screaming hideously and clawing dementedly at the blood-soaked area around his groin. His clothing there was tattered from the many bullets that had torn through it and there appeared to be nothing left between his legs except a hash of torn flesh.

Deeply shocked for the first time in years, Jacko tried to block out his mate's dreadful screams and instead gave his anger free rein as he fired off a sustained, savage burst that sent bullets ricocheting noisily off the bicycles and caused their riders to topple over like skittles.

'Kill me! Kill me! Kill me!' Harry-boy suddenly started screaming as he slithered over the ground, clawing frantically at his bloody groin. 'Ah, Jesus! Oh, God!'

Mercifully, a burst from a German sub-machine-gun kicked the dirt up around him, then stitched right over him, blowing off most of his head and punching his body full of holes. He shuddered violently while the bullets were stitching him, then froze and went quiet.

Outraged, Jacko fired another ferocious burst from his Sten gun, then hurled a 36 hand-grenade. It landed in the midst of a group of five Germans who had leapt back on their bicycles and were attempting to escape up the hill. The explosion sent men and bicycles flying, the former hitting the ground like charred, shredded dolls and the bicycles buckling and, in one instance, falling to pieces, with a wheel spinning away down the hill towards the square. Jacko's grenade was quickly followed by a similar device thrown by Rich, then by a stolen German potato-masher hurled by Neil. The three grenades went off almost simultaneously, causing an ear-splitting cacophony and wreaking havoc among the dazed, bloodied Germans. Even as those untouched were running away in both directions, leaving their bicycles behind, Jacko, Rich and Neil were mercilessly cutting them down in a sustained hail of bullets. The few who actually managed to escape were then finished off by the SAS men and Maquisards taking control of both ends of the street.

While this was happening, Greaves and Lorrimer were leading a foot patrol round the east side of Châtillon, where the only firing that could be heard was taking place behind them in the town itself. Nevertheless, isolated groups of Germans were to be seen everywhere and Greaves's group soon found themselves following four escaping Panzer troops over the crest of a low hill and into a copse of beech trees. When the Germans stopped to study a map of the area, arguing in a whisper among themselves, the SAS men all opened fire at once, swiftly dispatching the Germans with a fusillade that peppered their backs before they could even turn around.

Marching in a large arc that would ensure they would not be found by any Germans who might have seen them entering the trees, Greaves's men emerged by a lock in the Seine, which partly encircled the town and château. Crossing the lock and walking along the side of the tow-path, hugging the hedgerows, well away from the exposed space by the river, they saw two more Panzer troops zigzagging at the crouch across a graveyard. Lorrimer, carrying a .303-inch Lee-Enfield, picked both Germans off with two well-placed shots, then the group moved on.

After walking for another five minutes they found themselves in the garden of a farmhouse beside a narrow lane which, they now realized, curved down in the direction of the Troyes-Chaumont crossroads. Clambering over the wall in the garden and inching carefully around the blind bend, they were surprised to see that German machine-gun posts had been established on each side of the Troyes road. Clearly they had been left there by an optimistic officer who had hoped to give protection to his fellow Panzer troops when they fled the city. Equally clearly, that officer had not returned and the machine-gun crew did not know that the few of their comrades still left alive were trapped in the streets and lanes of the town.

The crew manning the guns, all wearing greatcoats and steel helmets, had their backs turned to the SAS men. Unable to think of what to do other than shoot the Germans in the back, in cold blood, Greaves and the others, not turned murderous with rage by witnessing the dreadful death of Harry-boy Turnball, decided to wait it out in the garden, assuming the Germans would leave eventually. When, after another thirty minutes, it became clear that the Germans were not likely to move for some time, Lorrimer boldly clambered back over the wall of the farm, hammered on the door of the farmhouse and, when the startled farmer's wife came out, charmed bread, cheese and a bottle of wine from her. Despite being forced to keep their eyes glued to the Germans below, the men enjoyed their light lunch enormously.

'Bloody good, that was,' Lorrimer said. 'But we can't sit here all day drinking wine and waiting for those bastards down there to leave. What say you, boss?'

'They're not going to surrender,' Greaves said, 'and I still don't like the idea of shooting them in the back.'

'We're not shooting them in the back in cold blood,' Lorrimer insisted. 'There's a battle going on and we've got to get rid of them somehow. Short of standing up and announcing our presence, giving them time to shoot us, I say shoot them now.'

'Actually,' Corporal Jim Almonds said, 'we'll only have to shoot one of them in the back. Once we do that, the others will turn around to face us and we can fire with clear consciences.'

'Our signaller is a pragmatist,' Lorrimer said, 'and I agree with him, boss.'

'Right,' Greaves said. 'Let's do it.'

'So who shoots the first man in the back?' Lorrimer asked.

'Let's toss for it,' Almonds suggested.

Impressed more every second by the normally reticent signaller, Greaves nodded and pulled a French franc from his pocket. After tossing it two or three times, with each man choosing heads or tails and candidates for the task gradually being eliminated, the loser turned out to be Lorrimer. As the sergeant was the best single-shot rifleman in C Squadron, he suspected that he had been fitted up by Greaves and told him so.

'What a low thing to think of me,' the captain replied with a mischievous grin. 'Now get on with it, Sergeant.'

Impatient to be getting back to town where, as the greatly diminished firing indicated, the mopping-up was nearly finished, Lorrimer wasted no more time and, taking careful aim with his Lee-Enfield, squeezed the trigger.

The single shot split the silence and the German in Lorrimer's sights jerked forward violently and fell on his face. Instantly galvanized into action, the other members of the gun crew swung their machine-guns and personal weapons round to aim up the hill. They were doing so as the rest of Greaves's group unleashed a fusillade down on them and had the pleasure of seeing some of the Germans jerk sideways or backwards, collapsing across their weapons.

Their pleasure was short-lived. Suddenly, Schmeissers and Spandaus roared from behind the hedgerow at the far side of, and lower down, the lane, sending bullets ricocheting noisily off the ground around the SAS men. Those bullets soon found their target, chopping down Sergeant Riley and Corporal Seekings, both of whom died instantly.

'I've been hit!' Corporal Almonds bawled, dropping his Lee-Enfield, staggering back a little, and clutching his bloody left upper arm. 'Fuck!'

'Over the wall!' Greaves yelled, shocked to learn so brutally that another large group of Germans had been camping in the field at the other side of the high hedgerow. Firing his Sten gun from the hip, he made his way backwards to the low stone wall bordering the farmer's garden, screaming as he went: 'Bug out! Withdraw! Over the wall!'

By now, the narrow, high-banked lane had become a virtual death-trap, with Schmeisser bullets whining between and around the SAS men, soon claiming another one of their number.

'Lance-Corporal Taggart down!' Lorrimer shouted into his S-phone, hoping that someone in the town would hear him and send reinforcements. 'Sergeant Riley and Corporal Seekings down! We're withdrawing right now!'

A Schmeisser bullet ricocheted off the S-phone container and went winging off into the blue, though its impact was enough to propel Lorrimer backwards into the wall, where he turned around and began clambering up the stones. He had just dropped down the other side when the man beside him, Trooper Phil Bellamy, grunted as if punched, then jerked forward and flopped face down on the grass with an enormous red stain spreading over the back of his bullet-riddled Denison smock. Knowing he was dead, Lorrimer saw no sense in picking him up and instead followed the others across the garden to the farmhouse as bullets continued to buzz angrily about them. More bullets were zipping off the white walls of the farmhouse, peppering it with ugly holes, as the SAS men kicked the front door open and rushed inside.

Waving and shouting apologies to the startled woman who had fed them, they ran straight through the living-room and kitchen, then out through the back door. Once outside, with the house between them and the Germans, they scrambled down the bank of the canal, then made their way back along the tow-path to the lock. Crossing the lock again, they headed towards Châtillon, thinking they were safe. But suddenly, in the middle of a ploughed field below the château, they heard the sound of a single Spandau.

Lorrimer yelped briefly and folded double.

'Damn!' he muttered, sitting up again and clutching his bloody left leg. 'I've been hit in the thigh.'

As two of the men poured a fusillade of submachine-gun fire in the direction from which they thought the Spandau was firing, Greaves swiftly knelt beside his sergeant, gave his bloody wound a cursory examination and said: 'It's just a flesh wound, my old mate, so you've no need to worry. I'll . . .'

He was cut off in mid sentence by the distant but unmistakable roaring of 9mm Sten guns. Abruptly the Spandau went silent. A few seconds later a green flare burst in the sky over where the men had suspected the Spandau was located. Greaves turned back to Lorrimer.

'Our boys,' he said. 'They've put the Spandau out of action.' Even as he spoke, the sounds of a vicious fire-fight exploded in the distance, in the direction of the Troyes–Chaumont crossroads. The battle raged for some time, then gradually faded away. When the last shot had been fired, another green flare exploded above the area of the intersection, indicating that the SAS were in control.

Indeed, green flares were exploding all over town and there were no more shots.

Châtillon was now in the hands of the SAS and the Maquis.

'Still,' Greaves said to Lorrimer, 'there might be the odd Kraut about, determined not to give in, so we'd better be careful. Do you think you can make it back to the town or shall I send someone back for you?'

'As long as I'm breathing I can make it,' Lorrimer replied in a defiant tone. 'I can crawl on my belly.'

'We'll all be doing that,' Greaves said.

This was true. In order to avoid any remaining German snipers, Greaves and the rest of his men, including the wounded sergeant, wriggled on their bellies along the furrows of the ploughed field until they reached a stretch of 'dead' ground which, being hollow, would shield them from gunfire. Once there, Lorrimer, weakened by loss of blood, let Greaves temporarily bandage his wound while two of the other men advanced at the crouch to recce what was in front of them. They returned a couple of minutes later to confirm that the town had been taken and that the only men in front of them were SAS and Maquis. Two of the former would be coming up any minute with a stretcher for Lorrimer.

In fact it was Callaghan who appeared in a jeep with Jacko, Rich and Neil, all of whom were distraught at the horrible death of their friend Harry-boy Turnball. Behind that jeep, however, was another jeep carrying a medic, two stretcher bearers and a stretcher. Lorrimer was rolled on to the stretcher, humped into the jeep and then driven back to the town, where the grateful Mayor had offered his large house as an emergency medical post.

Setting up a temporary command post in the post office in the market square, the three SAS officers, Callaghan, Greaves and Lazenby, conferred with André Flaubert and Maxine, to learn that between them the SAS and the Maquis had killed over a hundred Germans and wounded many more. They had also destroyed many German vehicles, including armoured cars, jeeps, motor-cycles and bicycles. The battle for Châtillon was over.

That evening, when the SAS men returned to their woodland hide, they heard over the No. 11 wireless set that General Patton's 3rd Army had taken Dijon earlier in the day.

There was no longer any need for night raids – or any other kind of raids – in that particular area. The SAS, with the help of the Maquis, had completed their task.

16

The SAS had picked up an inaccurate report about the fall of Dijon. In fact, it was French troops who liberated Dijon on 11 September 1944. On the same day the first waves of General Patch's 7th Army, having advanced 350 miles in slightly less than a month, made contact with General Patton's US 3rd Army at Sombernon, west of Dijon. Later that day, Patton and a contingent of his men made the short journey to Dijon, where they met up with the French and secured the city.

SAS operations in France, Belgium, the Netherlands and. Germany continued right up until the unconditional surrender of the Germans on 4 May 1945. During that time the SAS killed approximately 2000 of the enemy, wounded over 7000, captured more than another 7000, and even negotiated the surrender of a further 18,000. In a total of 164 raids they also destroyed 700 vehicles and seven trains, derailed a further thirty-three trains and cut numerous railway lines. Last but not least, they reported many bombing targets to the Allies and otherwise supplied them with a wealth of invaluable intelligence.

The price paid for these achievements was 330 reported casualties, including the deaths of many French civilians and

Maquisards, who were tortured and shot for assisting the SAS. So successful were the SAS in harassing the Germans that Hitler ordered captured SAS men to be tortured and then put to death. The exact number of SAS dead has never been revealed.

The SAS was officially disbanded in October 1945. A month later the SAS Regimental Association was formed. Then, in 1947, the War Office established a Territorial Army raiding unit which was attached to the Rifle Brigade, a unit that merged with the Artists Rifles, the latter raised in 1859 as a volunteer battalion and known in 1947 as 21 SAS (Artists). In 1950, Brigadier Mike 'Mad Mike' Calvert, a Chindit and SAS commander during World War Two, was called upon for a solution to the Malayan Emergency and suggested the creation of a special military force able to operate independently for long periods in the jungle. His recommendation led to the formation of the Malaya Scouts and a detachment from 21 SAS (Artists) soon joined them. Following the initial success of the Malaya Scouts, 22 SAS was formed out of them in 1952.

The Group's HQ was located in the Duke of York's Barracks, London, and the regimental base was Bradbury Lines, Merebrooke Camp, Malvern, Worcestershire, where it remained until 1960, when it was moved to Hereford.

Many of the Originals who had been founder members of L Detachment, SAS Brigade, in 1941 and fought in north-west Europe, went on to fight more major campaigns in Malaya, Borneo, Oman and Aden throughout the 1950s and '60s. Some were killed in action, others wounded so badly that they could not serve again, and yet others, when the inexorable passage of time rendered them too old for active duty, went on to become drill instructors and teachers at the

Training Wing, Counter Revolutionary Warfare Wing, Demolitions Wing or 264 SAS Signals at Bradbury Lines and, later, Stirling Lines, Hereford; or intelligence officers and strategists at Operations Research Wing or Operations Planning and Intelligence, known as 'the Kremlin'.

The lessons learnt by the Originals, and the tactics and skills developed as a consequence of those lessons during their first forays into the North African desert with the Long Range Desert Group and, later, during their many day and night raids against the Germans in Europe, stood them in good stead in the future and were constantly revised to accommodate new kinds of warfare and the introduction of more sophisticated weapons and technical equipment, particularly in the areas of communications and surveillance. It was therefore no accident that, after the North African campaigns and the battles in north-west Europe, the SAS should find themselves being used over the years for sabotage, intelligence-gathering missions, 'hearts-and-minds' campaigns, long-range reconnaissance, clandestine insertion, Counter Insurgency (COIN) and Counter Revolutionary Warfare (CRW) in locations as diverse as the Far East, the Middle East, Northern Ireland, the Falkland Islands, and Iraq.

At least once a year the SAS Originals of World War Two – some retired from the regiment, others scattered throughout its many wings and camps, and yet others, mostly officers, returned to their original units – would have a reunion at which they would fondly reminisce about what most of them believed were, if not the most spectacular, then certainly the most romantic days of the SAS: the early years in North Africa and north-west Europe.

During such boozy, noisy reunions, the Originals, their numbers diminishing annually through death from both 'natural' and 'unnatural' causes, would mock their own heroic or foolish acts and make jokes about old mates. They always made a point, however, of never mentioning the names of those who had failed to return. Those names were taboo.

And yet the dead were not forgotten. The names of those who died in action were inscribed on plaques originally attached to the base of the Regimental Clock Tower at Bradbury Lines. For this reason, 'beating the clock' became SAS slang for staying alive. When the new barracks block, Stirling Lines, was complete in 1960, the plaques were resited outside the Regimental Chapel, but by now the term was well and truly established in SAS parlance.

Even though the names of the dead were rarely, if ever, heard among the SAS, they lived on in the collective memory of the regiment. They were part of SAS history and duly honoured in silence.